Praise for
First Star I See

"Jaye Caffrey has created a wonderful adventure packed with great information on TWO topics. After readers finish this book, they will be much more informed about the nature of ADD and what it's like to live daily with the struggles of forgetfulness and disorganization. On top of that, *First Star I See* is a well-researched study on the nature of stars and space. All this packed into one fast-moving book is sure to capture the hearts and minds of readers of all ages."
—*Dorothy Leal, Assistant Professor, College of Education, Ohio University, Athens, Ohio*

"Readers feel the hurt and frustration of a bright young girl who does not have the tools to focus her energy and intellect. I can see using this book in a counseling situation with children who have ADD or others who do not have ADD but need to understand and empathize with children who do."
—*Joanne Fulton, ACSW, LCSW, Social Work Department, William Woods University, Missouri*

"*First Star I See* informs and entertains readers regardless of their personal knowledge of ADD."
—*Stephanie Borgman, Children's Librarian, Houston, Texas*

ISBN 1-884281-17-6
Copyright © 1997 by Jaye Andras Caffrey
Cover and inside illustrations copyright © 1997 by Verbal Images Press
Printed in the United States of America

Publisher's Cataloging in Publication
Caffrey, Jaye Andras
    First star I see by Jaye Andras Caffrey: illustrated by Tracy L. Kane.
    160 p.   19 cm
    Summary: Trying to win a school writing contest helps bright, imaginative Paige Bradley realize that fixing her "focusing knob" will compensate for her ADD.

1. Attention Deficit Disorder-Juvenile fiction. 2. Family Relationships-Juvenile fiction. 3. Schools-Juvenile fiction. [1. Attention Deficit Disorder-Fiction. 2. Family Relationships-Fiction. 3. Schools-Fiction.] I. Kane, Tracy L., ill. II. Title

ISBN 1-884281-17-6
[Fic] - dc20

A word about terminology:
At the time of this publication, medical researchers use many different terms to describe the condition known as attention deficit disorder (ADD). Numerous acronyms differentiate between people who have hyperactivity (such as ADHD, ADDH, etc.) and those who don't (for example, undifferentiated ADD, ADD w/o, and others). In this work of fiction for children, we have chosen to avoid the ever-evolving acronyms and use the simple terms "ADD without hyperactivity" to characterize Paige Bradley and "ADD with hyperactivity" to describe her brother Mark.

Verbal Images Press
19 Fox Hill Drive • Fairport, New York 14450
(716) 377-3807 • Fax (716) 377-5401

Table of Contents

Grateful Acknowledgments:

☆ To my wonderful family: Evan and Emma Caffrey and Michael Bardwell; my mother Pat Fenerty and my father Bob Andras, who is always there for me when I need him and who appreciates the humor in everyday life.

☆ To the librarians and other good souls who have given so generously of themselves: Taylor Aultman, Wester Perrett, Virginia Deputy, Patti Towbin, and Jeanne Gehret. —J.A.C.

1
Space Academy

Did you ever want something so bad that you'd trade all your Christmas and birthday presents for it? Or let your little brother have control of the TV remote for an entire year? Well, that's how I felt the day that our teacher, Mrs. Bourgeois, made the big announcement.

"Okay, fourth graders," Mrs. Bourgeois (whose name is pronounced "Buj-wa") said at the end of reading period, "I have some exciting news for you. Eyes to the front of the room, please." The sound of scraping chairs and slamming books filled the room as the kids settled down to listen.

"Paige Bradley, will you please stop talking and pay attention?"

I stifled the comment I was whispering to my best friend, Breanna Barnett, who sits right in front of me. Usually we don't get caught. That's because Mrs. Bourgeois can't hear or see very well. She wears a hearing aid and strange oval glasses. She's ancient (at least fifty years old) and although she's not the oldest teacher at Sylvia Probst

Elementary School in New Orleans, she is certainly one of the stone-agers.

I was just about to tell Breanna that I was tired of listening to snobby Jessica Patino, who sits right behind me, bragging to her best friend, Pauline Smith. Jessica talks constantly about all the Barbies she already has and

all the new ones her dad is going to get for her. She and Pauline think they're awesome because they are pretty and popular and because Jessica has practically every Barbie toy there is.

Unfortunately, those two don't like me at all. Ever since school started, I have earned a reputation for being "spacey." That's what Jessica and Pauline call me when I get caught daydreaming, or forget my homework, or misplace my pencil. They especially tease me about never being able to find my school supplies when I need them.

I don't know how it happens, but somehow my stuff just seems to disappear into thin air! One minute I know where my markers or my scissors are, and the next minute, they're gone!

3

When Mrs. Bourgeois saw my eyes fixed on her, she continued, "Now, children. I have a treat for you in connection with this month's work on the Solar System."

Heads bobbed up and down while students tried to see what the surprise was. Was it on her desk? No, nothing unusual there.

Well, no—that wasn't exactly true, I realized. Mrs. Bourgeois' fat brown purse was on top of her desk, instead of in her drawer, where she usually kept it. It reminded me of the day we had that awful substitute with the high, squeaky voice. (I have to admit that we kids were pretty tough on her.)

Right before she stormed out of the room in the middle of fourth period, she pulled her purse out of the desk drawer and plunked it on the desk. Leaning towards us, she glared and squeaked, "That's it! I quit! You children are monsters!" Unfortunately, she sounded just like a mouse with its tail caught in a mousetrap. We fell all over ourselves laughing. Our principal, Mrs. Martin, taught the class for the rest of the day, and we were all in big trouble!

Now, as I looked at Mrs. Bourgeois' purse sitting there on the desk, it suddenly dawned on me: Mrs. Bourgeois was quitting!

I looked at her in alarm. I didn't want Mrs. Bourgeois

to quit. I mean, it was already April, and it had taken me most of the school year to get used to her! Even though she made us work hard, Mrs. Bourgeois didn't assign nearly as much homework as Mrs. Evans gave the other fourth grade class. A new teacher could be worse. She could have better hearing.

I tried to listen. Mrs. Bourgeois was saying something about an astronaut. An astronaut? Was she leaving us to become a teacher in space? Maybe the government was sending her to teach reading, writing, and math to ten-eyed, eight-armed, three-legged Martian children.

I could just see Mrs. Bourgeois in a space suit making the little Martians line up by twos for recess. "Eyes to the front of the room!" she would order. The Martians would begin spinning around and knocking each other over trying to get all of their eyes focused on the front of the room at the same time.

I began to giggle.

"What is so funny, Paige Bradley?" Mrs. Bourgeois asked sternly. I looked up, gulping. Everyone stared at me.

I could have said "nothing," but no, I decided to explain. That was a fatal mistake. "Well, you see, Mrs. Bourgeois, it was the little Martians," I began. "They were trying to do what you wanted them to do but, um . . . . they

5

were falling over. You know, they have so many eyes, on those little antenna things." A couple of kids started laughing. I felt my face getting red.

"The little Martians . . . ?" Mrs. Bourgeois looked puzzled.

"Well, you see, your purse was on your desk. And I um . . . ." The whole class was roaring now. I gave up; it was hopeless.

Jessica said loudly, "Spacey was daydreaming again!" I cringed.

However, Mrs. Bourgeois stared at me, puzzled. "What about my purse?" She started to say something else, then shrugged. Pulling an index card out of her purse, she explained, "I was just getting some notes I need about our special assembly in three weeks."

When most of the kids had stopped snickering, she continued, "As all of you are aware, we have been studying the lives of several famous astronauts in connection with our unit on space and space travel. Most recently we learned about Dr. Sally Ride. Next, we will move on to study the solar system and our galaxy."

"Now," she went on, "I have decided to assign to each of you a research paper on our theme. The paper with the highest grade will be presented by its author to the entire school at an assembly. In addition, a student from each of the other classes will also be presenting a paper, and Mrs. Martin has decided that there is to be a school-wide competition for the best report."

Big deal! I thought, disappointed. Is that all?

But as Mrs. Bourgeois continued, her voice rose with excitement. "At the assembly we will have a very special guest judge to select the best paper. Finally, our class has been selected to decorate the big bulletin board in the entry hall with a Milky Way. The bulletin board will be a fine showcase of our work for the entire school to see." Mrs. Bourgeois beamed at us proudly as if the last bit of news was a great accomplishment.

"You mean we're going to decorate the bulletin board with candy bars?" Keith Guidry piped up. Keith was the baddest, goofiest, and worst-smelling boy in the whole class; he sat next to me. Sometimes he called Mrs. Bourgeois "Mrs. Bushwhack." Luckily for him, she couldn't hear well enough to tell the difference! He spent so much of his day in the time-out chair that the class called it the "Keith Guidry Memorial Chair."

Unlike me, Keith didn't seem to mind time-out at all. There he sat in front of everybody, all red spiky hair and freckles, mugging and making faces at Will Schiffer, his best friend. On top of that, he'd do just about anything to get people to notice him. I bet Keith Guidry would have come to school dressed only in his underwear for ten dollars. No, make that ten cents.

"Don't be silly, Keith," Mrs. Bourgeois said sternly. "Construction paper and Styrofoam balls. I hope you will take this project seriously because this is a great honor and . . . ."

"Mrs. Bourgeois," Carol Collins raised her hand insistently. She was the teacher's pet and always said the right thing at the right time. "Who is the guest judge, and what's the special prize?"

"Oh, dear me, did I forget to tell you that?" said Mrs. Bourgeois. "She's a famous TV actor. At least that's what Mrs. Martin says . . . *I've* never heard of this person. Let's see . . ." she hesitated, peering down through her thick glasses at the index card in her hand. "Are any of you familiar with the TV show called *Star Warrior?*"

Had we heard of it? Was she kidding? Everybody in the room sat up straight suddenly, excited. *Star Warrior,* of course, is the best, most awesome TV show ever. Breanna and I had never missed an episode.

Mrs. Bourgeois went on. "One of the actors from the show is related to Mr. Hubble, the kindergarten teacher.

The actor will be in town for a family reunion, and Mr. Hubble has arranged for that person to visit the school and judge our competition." Mrs. Bourgeois peered nearsightedly at the card in her hand, completely unaware of our excitement.

"Oh, please let it be Dr. Kelsey!" Breanna whispered.

"It's just got to be!" I whispered back. Dr. Kelsey was the beautiful, brave heroine of *Star Warrior*. Breanna and I played *Star Warrior* every recess, and whenever Breanna came to play at my house, we took turns being Dr. Kelsey Strongheart, the beautiful heroine. Sometimes we played with our Barbies and pretended that Flying Angel Barbie was Dr. Kelsey and that Fantasy Date Ken was Captain Stone Griffith, her handsome astronaut boyfriend.

We got our wish! "The actor," Mrs. Bourgeois said, "is a . . . . Renee . . . . La Straps, who plays Dr. Kelsey. The actress will personally present an autographed picture of herself at the assembly, as well as a . . . . virtual crysto-laser. Yes, I think that's what this says, a . . . virtual crysto-laser, to the student who has given the best presentation."

"Oooh, I want to meet her!" exclaimed Jessica. "Will we get to talk to her, Mrs. Bourgeois?"

"Only one or two children will have that privilege," replied our teacher. "Renee La Straps has to leave right after the assembly, and only one of you—that is, the student with the highest grade—will be on the stage with her." She smiled. "So if you really want to meet her, do a good job on your paper!"

Breanna turned around, eyes wide, mouth hanging open. "Did you hear that?" she gasped. "Dr. Kelsey is coming to *our* school!"

"I heard it," I said, shaking my head in wonderment. "But I can hardly believe it!" Right then and there, I knew I wanted to win that prize more than anything else in the whole world. I just had to write the best paper. I imagined Dr. Kelsey pinning the virtual crysto-laser on my shirt in front of everyone at Sylvia Probst Elementary School. Nobody would ever call me "spacey" again.

"I want to win so bad!" I sighed out loud.

Jessica heard me. She turned around to Pauline and giggled. "As *if!*" she said. "Anyway, Pauline and I are the best writers in this class. One of us is sure to win. Hey, Pauline," she said, turning to her friend. "Let's pledge each other, here and now, that whoever wins, we'll share the crysto-laser with the other. Deal?"

Nodding excitedly and shaking Jessica's hand, Pauline said, "Deal!"

Breanna turned around and gave me a look that said,

"Can you believe how stuck up they are?" I made a gagging motion with my finger and rolled my eyes. But when Breanna turned around again I felt a momentary uneasiness. What if Jessica was right? . . . No! I thought. I can do this. I can. I don't know how, but I've just got to win that contest!

2
Peevers and Other Crew Mates

After lunch, Mrs. Bourgeois assigned us topics for our research papers. Planets went to the first nine children, with Jessica getting Earth. (Somehow, that didn't seem fair.) Will Schiffer was eighth, and he got Neptune. After Breanna was assigned Pluto, the next eight kids got the sun, moon, asteroids, meteoroids, comets, constellations, satellites, and telescopes. Finally, she assigned stars to me.

Stars! I thought. I've got a head start! After all, Breanna and I have seen every single episode of *Star Warrior* at least once.

That, of course, is just one of the reasons I like Breanna so much. Another reason is that, unlike Jessica, Breanna doesn't think I'm dumb. In fact, she says I'm funny and that I have good ideas. She has pretty, black hair, which she wears in cornrows or a ponytail, with bangs like mine. (My hair, however, is curly brown and "impossible," according to my mom.)

Breanna is also very smart, and she almost never gets in trouble.

Unlike me.

Take what happened in geography class, for instance. Later that day, Mrs. Bourgeois told us to use colored pencils to make a map of the United States as part of our geography lesson. Somewhere between Mississippi and Texas I slipped into my own thoughts. I decided to add the state capitols for extra credit.

Then I found that if you added a few extra capitols in the right places, it made a beautiful web, especially if you marked them with stars. Hmmm. Stars reminded me of the opening scene of my favorite program . . . . I started thinking about Dr. Kelsey sitting on the auditorium stage with the virtual crysto-laser in her lap. I imagined sitting right next to her and thinking of what I would say to her. I lifted my head, brushed my bangs out of my eyes, and leaned back in my seat to admire my star-spangled country.

"Paige." Seeing Mrs. Bourgeois standing over my desk made me jump. I hadn't even noticed her coming.

"Uh . . . . yes, ma'am?" Full of dread, I waited for her to say something about the map, but she didn't.

"I'd like for you to go see Mr. Rodriguez." Turning around halfway, Breanna flashed me a sympathetic look.

My heart sank. I must really be in trouble. Mr. Rodriguez is the assistant principal. Actually, if I wasn't in trouble, going to see him would not have been so bad. He's tall with black hair and kind, dark eyes, and Breanna thinks he looks just like Captain Stone Griffith. If you squint at him a certain way, he kind of does. We used to pretend that he really *was* Captain Stone, and one day Breanna even wrote in the dust on his car window "BB loves CSG" (for Captain Stone Griffith).

Nevertheless, this trip to see him could mean nothing but bad news. What had I done wrong? I tried to read Mrs. Bourgeois' face. However, she didn't look like she was upset with me at all; in fact, she looked like she was trying to be nice.

I could hear the kids whispering, "Paige is being sent to see Mr. Rodriguez!"

"Um . . . . go see Mr. Rodriguez? Why?" I whispered, stalling for time. My heart started to beat faster. "Is it because I didn't do my map right?"

Mrs. Bourgeois looked down at my work and frowned, but she said, "No, Paige. He would like to have a little talk with you. He'll send you right back to class when you're done."

The teacher stood there waiting. It was no use! I got up

14

feeling like I was going off to my doom, just like Dr. Kelsey must have felt that time when she was on Planet Priamus and she allowed the Grumblions to capture her in order to save the star fleet. I walked as slowly as possible to the school office, trying desperately to think what I could have done.

"Sit there," said Mrs. Landry, the school secretary, when I finally walked into the office. She pointed to an old wooden bench next to Mr. Rodriguez's door. I obeyed quietly. Mrs. Landry was a fat, blonde lady with painted-on eyebrows. She returned to typing on her computer keyboard and ignored me.

I was glad. I chewed on my fingernails and, even though I knew I wasn't supposed to, bumped my feet against the bench. What difference did it make now, anyway? After all, I was dead meat as soon as Mom found out I had been sent to the office. What on earth did I do? I felt like my dog Peevers waiting for the "thwack!" of the newspaper after she left a present on the living room rug.

Thinking of Peevers cheered me up some. She's a good-natured, but goofy, Labrador mix that Dad brought home the week before he left to live with his girlfriend Susan. My little brother, Mark, and I fell in love with her right away. Peevers had big chocolate eyes and soft brown fur and was even more hyper than Mark. (If you knew my little brother, you'd know why I didn't even think that was possible at first!)

But even as I let the puppy tug at my shoelaces and lick my chin, I knew Mom would send it packing with Dad. After all, he had violated that First Rule of Mothers, which neither Mark nor I had ever been able to get around: Don't bring pets home without consulting Mom first.

Luckily for Mark and me, Susan refused to take the dog.

"I don't believe that man!" stormed Mom after she got off the phone with Dad that afternoon. "He expects *me* to take a pet that his *girlfriend* doesn't want!" She threw down the dish towel she was holding and kicked it angrily.

Later, when she had calmed down, Mark and I pleaded to keep the pup. Mom finally gave in, saying we might need a watchdog, and muttered that we were getting a "better deal than poor Susan."

Mom started calling the puppy "My Pet Peeve," explaining that a "pet peeve" is the most annoying thing that you can imagine. Before long, our new puppy's name was shortened to "Peevers."

I was in first grade when Dad moved out and Peevers moved in. Until that year, we lived in a big two-story brick house on Pecan Street in New Orleans. There, Mark (who was only three at the time) and I each had our own room and shared a playroom for our toys. Peevers lived in the house with us but could go in and out of the house through a doggy door leading to our big back yard which was surrounded by a brick wall that was fun to balance on when Mom wasn't looking.

All in all, it was a pretty rotten year for our family. Right before Christmas that year, Mom was laid off from her job at Hansen's Antique Shop. She decided to go back to finish her college degree, but even after she had graduated, she couldn't find a job. So Mom, Mark and I moved to Milton Street, to a little wooden house that needed lots of repairs. There, my brother and I had to share a bedroom, and we had no playroom. A rusty chain link fence surrounded the back yard. Using the excuse that our new house was too small, Mom insisted from day one that Peevers move out of the house and into the fenced area.

But Peevers just hated that yard. As soon as we put her back there and closed the gate, she dug a hole under the chain link and made her escape. After trying lots of tricks to keep Peevers penned in, Mom sort of gave up.

Peevers took advantage of her new freedom to become Milton Street's most notorious criminal—a real toy thief.

She regularly stalked kids playing outside with their toys, waiting for her chance to strike.

Here's how she did it. First, she picked some poor unsuspecting victim like William Clementson from down the block. William would be innocently playing with his action figures in the dirt in front of his house, happily unaware of approaching danger. Peevers went slinking through the hydrangea bushes until she was just a few paw widths away. Then she rushed the poor kid, jumping around, licking his hand, and pretending she wanted to play. No kid could resist her . . . . but it was a trap!

As soon as William put his toy down to pet Peevers, it was no-more-Miss-Nice-Dog. She pounced. With the toy clenched in her jaws, she took off like a furry rocket. William followed, screaming, straight to our back yard where Peevers had started to bury her loot.

To break Peevers of this habit, Mom tried everything, including thwacking Peevers with *The Times-Picayune* newspaper. But the dog seemed determined to create her own little toy cemetery in our back yard. Not even the Sunday paper could stop her!

I was thinking so hard about Peevers that I forgot I was waiting to see the assistant principal. When Mr. Rodriguez' door opened suddenly, I jumped. A fifth-grade boy emerged with a black eye and a torn shirt. His good eye looked red, as if he'd been crying. I knew how he felt. The tear ducts in my eyes started to sting as I wondered what my own punishment would be.

3
Captain Stone Griffith Joins the Crew

"Mrs. Landry, Shawn's parents will arrive in a moment to pick him up. He's had a rough day." Mr. Rodriguez patted Shawn on the back, adding, "Sit here, son." Turning to where I sat, the assistant principal noticed me for the first time. "Hi, Paige, come on in."

On shaky legs, I followed him into his small, crowded office. I liked it right away. Even though I still felt very nervous, I tried to remember what it looked like so I could tell Breanna.

There was a basketball hoop over the window, which was covered with cartoon-character curtains. Pinned to the bulletin board behind the desk were dozens of cartoon strips cut from newspapers. In addition to many books, the bookshelves also held trophies, little statues, and photographs. On the ceiling was a black poster, covered with what seemed like zillions of tiny silver dots.

But I found myself fascinated with a stand holding a

long, dark tube that poked stiffly through the curtains.

"Do you like my telescope?" asked Mr. Rodriguez, noticing my gaze.

"Yes, sir," I said, sitting on the edge of the chair he offered. "But why do you have it in here? Do you use it to spy on kids on the playground?" Instantly, I felt bad about having said that. Mr. Rodriguez seemed friendly enough. Why had I insulted him?

But he laughed. "Well, I could. That's a pretty good idea." He sat down behind his desk. "I just like to watch the stars at night when I work late. I have another one at home."

I suddenly remembered that I'd been called to his office for something serious. "Are you going to call my mother?" I asked, jumping right to the point.

"Actually," said Mr. Rodriguez, "I've already called her." I must have looked upset because he said, "Cheer up. You haven't done anything wrong."

"I haven't? Then why am I here?"

"Well, this may sound silly but . . . . Mrs. Bourgeois wanted me to ask you about the little green Martians in her purse. What *is* she talking about, Paige?" Mr. Rodriguez leaned forward with his chin in his hand, studying my face.

I giggled with relief and tried to explain. When I

finished, I peeked at Mr. Rodriguez through my bangs to see if he understood.

He smiled and said, "I get the picture. So, Paige, you didn't think you saw *real* Martians, right?"

"No, of course not! I was just imagining, that's all. Did Mrs. Bourgeois think I meant real Martians?"

"Well . . . . I'm not sure. She did say you daydream a lot. Is that true?"

"Kind of. It isn't like I plan to start imagining stuff, except when I'm playing. Otherwise, it happens by itself. I just forget what I'm supposed to be doing. That's when I get in trouble."

"You know, Paige, it's very important to pay attention in class. Your teacher is worried about you. She says you're very smart and not working up to your potential."

"Worried about me?" I echoed doubtfully. "Sometimes I don't think she even likes me anymore. She always seems to be frowning when she looks at me, and she constantly says stuff like, 'Paige, are you with us? ' and 'Paige, you will not find the answer to the question outside the window' and 'Paige, for the hundredth time, pay attention, please!'" I did such a pretty good impression of Mrs. Bourgeois' old-lady voice that Mr. Rodriguez smiled. "I'm pretty sure she doesn't like me." I sighed.

"Oh, no," said Mr. Rodriguez firmly, "you're wrong about that. She likes you a lot, and she wants you to pay attention and finish your work. She thinks you're not trying because she believes you can do the assignments when you try. She's concerned that you're not focusing on your work consistently, not applying yourself."

I sighed, slouching in my seat a little. "That's what my dad says, too—that I just don't apply myself. I wish I could figure out *how* to, but I don't even know what it means." I looked at the assistant principal, not sure that even I understood how things in my life always got so messed up.

"Do you ever imagine stuff, Mr. Rodriguez?" I asked.

"Sure. Sometimes, when I get stuck for an idea, I even

do it on purpose. I just lean back in my chair here and look up at my map of the stars." Mr. Rodriguez pointed to the ceiling. "That's when I do some of my best thinking."

I looked at the poster and realized that it was a map.

"Actually, it's good to be able to daydream," said Mr. Rodriguez. "The trick is knowing when and where to do it. It's not a good idea to let your thoughts wander too much in school. Do you have any special place at home where you can daydream?"

"Yes," I said, picturing my favorite spot immediately. "There's an old tree in my front yard, close to the sidewalk. It has big, twisted roots that have tunneled under the cement and broken it up. You have to be awfully careful not to trip when you walk there. The tree is so big that it makes a lot of shade and no grass grows under it." He nodded, interested, so I went on.

"Do you know what I did? I tied an old blanket between two strong branches to make a hammock. It's the most wonderful place in the world to lie and imagine things. The tree is perfect for climbing, with knots in all the right places. Did you like to climb trees when you were a kid?"

"Sure," he said. "In fact, I'll tell you a secret." He leaned towards me. "I would still climb trees if I didn't think other grown-ups would give me a hard time about it." I knew then that Mr. Rodriguez was just as cool as Captain Stone.

"So you like to sit in this tree and think?" he continued.

I nodded, adding shyly, "Sometimes I feel like that tree is just as good a friend as my best friend Breanna. Sometimes I talk to my tree. But I whisper so people don't think I'm crazy."

"And the tree doesn't answer back. Right?" Mr. Rodriguez smiled at me.

"No," I giggled. "But I still like to think she understands. It makes me feel better sometimes."

"I know what you mean," he said. "I had a stuffed toy that understood me when I was a kid. Now I just talk to the stars."

"And the stars don't answer back. Right?"

Mr. Rodriguez laughed. "Right."

"Hey . . . . stars!" I suddenly sat up straight. "That's what I have to do my paper on," I said excitedly, remembering. "Mrs. Bourgeois assigned each kid in my class a paper. The one who has the best paper gets to sit on the stage with Dr. Kelsey . . . . I mean, Renee La Straps! That's Dr. Kelsey's real name, you know! She's coming to our school! The real Dr. Kelsey Strongheart!"

Mr. Rodriguez smiled. "Yes, I've heard. Mrs. Martin is busy planning. It's all anybody has been talking about since I got here this morning."

"I'm going to do the best paper in my class!" I told him. "I want to meet Dr. Kelsey more than anything else in the whole world! Do you ever watch *Star Warrior*, Mr. Rodriguez? Don't you think it's awesome?"

"Oh, yes," said Mr. Rodriguez. "I know all about it. It's my kids' favorite show."

Suddenly I remembered something else. "Mr. Rodriguez, you said you already called my mother. What did you talk to her about?"

"Well," he replied, pausing, "I asked her how you were doing at home and if she thought you might really be the kind of kid who sees little green men."

"Was she upset?" I asked.

"No, she seemed to find it rather funny. I hope you don't mind, but she told me about Dr. Learner and her diagnosis."

I froze. My mom told him that! How could she? Did she want people to think I was crazy? It was bad enough being called spacey.

Mr. Rodriguez didn't seem to notice my frown. He went on. "She said that she took you to see a psychologist,

Dr. Learner, and that the psychologist says that you have attention deficit disorder, the kind where you sit still and daydream a lot." He paused. "Your mom says she's already explained to you about ADD, Paige. How do *you* feel about all this?"

How did I feel about it? . . . Mad! Attention deficit disorder (which my mom mostly just calls "ADD") is something my hyper little brother has, not me! Dr. Learner is Mark's psychologist. She helps him learn to control himself. But I'm nothing like my little brother.

"It's definitely not true!" I said. "My dad says it isn't. Anyway, it's all Mrs. Keller's fault that my mom made me go to that doctor. I'm definitely not hyper like Mark is."

Mrs. Keller was my third grade teacher. Even now, a year later, I still blushed when I thought of the math paper that she made such a big deal about. During a quiz on times tables, my mind started to wander, and I decorated the answer sheet with this awesome picture of a princess at a ball. Wearing a sparkly gown made of multiplication signs, she was taking turns dancing with handsome multiples of the number five, all dressed in tuxedos made of division signs.

That day I was brought back to the classroom by the sound of Mrs. Keller's slightly hysterical voice, as she stood over my desk. "Paige, what on earth are you doing to your math test?" she exclaimed. I looked up. The whole class was laughing. It was one of the most embarrassing moments of my whole life, and Jessica and Pauline seem to bring it up at least once a month and probably will do so forever. It's one of the reasons that I am considering moving to China when I grow up.

As if reading my mind, Mr. Rodriguez went on, "Mrs. Bourgeois pulled out an old math quiz of yours with drawings that you did when you were in Mrs. Keller's class last year. Remember?"

I nodded and let out a heavy sigh. "Mom says Mrs. Keller reminded her about that at every single parent-teacher conference last year. I think she convinced my mom that I'm pretty dumb."

"Dumb? Absolutely not!" said Mr. Rodriguez. "Your mother and I agree that you are smart and creative and have a very good imagination. Mrs. Bourgeois does, too, and I suspect Mrs. Keller thought as much."

Mr. Rodriguez went on, but I was savoring the words "smart," "creative," and "good imagination" like a delicious ice cream cone. After all, I didn't hear that kind of stuff too often. Was he telling the truth, or just trying to make me feel good? If Mrs. Bourgeois thought I was so smart, then why was she always scolding me? Just like Mrs. Keller did last year.

Mr. Rodriguez was still talking about that awful math test. I wondered if somehow they knew about it in China.

"Your math quiz artwork actually just shows how imaginative you can be!" he said. "But daydreaming can get you into trouble, can't it?"

"Daydreaming shouldn't be a crime, Mr. Rodriguez!" I protested sadly.

"Paige . . . . " Mr. Rodriguez waited until I looked up before he continued. "We want to help you be the best Paige you can be. It's harder for some students to do things like planning and paying attention than it is for others. They might just come more naturally to other kids."

"My dad says that I can pay attention when I want to," I said. "After all, he says that I would watch *Star Warrior* all day, every day, if I could. That's true, I would— because it's important to me. You know, it's kind of like this Dr. Kelsey thing: I want to meet her so much that I know I'm going to work very hard on my paper. I'm going to apply myself this time."

Mr. Rodriguez scratched his chin. "Well," he said, "I believe you. Have you given any thought to how you are going to approach this paper? What will you do first?"

"I don't know—I guess I'll just do it."

Mr. Rodriguez, however, was determined to talk about *how* I would do it. "Did Mrs. Bourgeois suggest an outline first, or does she just want the finished product right before the assembly?"

"I can't remember exactly . . . . but it can't be shorter than three pages, and she wants illustrations. I think that an outline is due this Friday and the draft next Friday." Anyway, there's three whole weeks until the actual paper is due. That's a long time."

"I have an idea," Mr. Rodriguez said thoughtfully. "I can see how much you want to meet Renee La Straps. If it turns out that, even with such a strong incentive, things don't go quite the way you want, well . . . . will you consider some other options?"

"Sure! No problem!"

"Good girl!" he said, standing up. "Now remember, if you have any trouble, come talk to me. You just tell Mrs. Landry that I said it was okay for you to come see me anytime. Anytime at all."

I blushed. The thought of being able to drop in on Mr. Rodriguez "anytime at all" made me feel pretty good. Maybe he liked me. I stole a glance at him as I got up to leave. He was shuffling papers around on his desk. Out of the corner of my eye he looked a lot like Captain Stone Griffith! Boy, was Breanna going to be impressed!

"Thanks, Mr. Rodriguez!" I called, skipping out of his office. "See you later!"

On the way back to class, though, I started to feel bad again. I couldn't believe my mom actually told Mr. Rodriguez about that ADD stuff. My dad would never have done that. I remembered when I told him about what Dr. Learner had said. He really hit the roof!

"What nonsense!" Dad said. "The only problem with you, Pumpkin, is that you don't apply yourself!"

"What does that mean—'apply myself'?" I asked.

"It just means that you don't try hard enough. But don't worry," Dad said. "Psychologists like Dr. Learner are not real doctors. They have to find something wrong with perfectly normal kids like you and Mark or else they can't get parents to pay them lots of money to play with their kids once a week. Mark is just high-spirited. He's a Tom Sawyer-type, that's all."

I'm not sure what "high spirited" means, but I'm pretty sure Tom Sawyer is a character on a television show my Dad liked when he was a kid. Anyway, no matter what Dad says, Mark really is hyper. His teachers are always calling Mom about him.

In preschool he ran all around the classroom during story hour. And during the first few weeks of kindergarten, his teacher complained that every time they did art he mixed all the paints together and snipped the construction paper into such tiny pieces that no one could use it. Once he gets started on an activity, though, there's no prying him away from it! Unless, of course, you offer him something better, like Mom does.

He used to do awful things at home, too. When Mark was two, Mom caught him walking across the very top bar of our swingset. One time when he was screaming about not wanting to go to bed, he bit her so hard that she bled. Ever since I can remember, he has wandered off in big stores, and we spend half our time looking for him. One time she got so worried she even called the store detectives! Boy, was that exciting! She acted so weird when they finally found him, though. She cried and hugged him, then spanked him and told him never to do that again.

I have to admit, though, that last year Mark started to change after Mom learned that he had the hyperactive-impulsive kind of ADD. Mom said ADD is why she has to tell Mark everything at least five times and why if we leave him alone for ten minutes, he'll rearrange all the furniture in the house or try to paint the dog blue. Or do something else that everybody in the whole world, except Mark, knows you shouldn't do.

Because of ADD, Mom started taking my brother to see Dr. Learner once a week. Since then his teacher hasn't called Mom nearly as often as she used to. At first, I kind of liked Dr. Learner because she helped Mark. But all that changed when Mrs. Keller talked my mom into taking me to see the doctor, too. When she said that I had the same disorder as Mark, I knew without a doubt . . . . she was a quack!

After Dad agreed with me, I told Mom that I was not going back to see Dr. Learner under any circumstances, no how, no way! My mom said she was disappointed that I didn't want to just check it out, but that she wouldn't force me to go.

4
In the Crew's Quarters

For dinner that night we had meat loaf, mashed potatoes, and peas—my favorite meal. I spoon the peas right on top of the mashed potatoes.

Mark hates peas. When Mom isn't looking, he hides them on top of the kitchen table's secret leaf—the kind that pops up when you pull the two sides of the table apart. Watching him, I told myself that I didn't want to be around the day we have company and Mom opens the table to find half of Mark's meals from the previous year.

Anyway, I told Mom all about Dr. Kelsey's visit and the paper we had to do. I even remembered to give her the note from Mrs. Bourgeois that listed the school supplies that I had lost recently.

"Crayons, pencils, glue . . . . " Mom read, brushing her shoulder-length brown hair away from her face. "Oh, Paige, please try to keep track of your belongings! I can't continue buying you new school supplies."

"I know," I said. "But I think there's a portal to an

alternate universe right next to my desk, just like in that *Star Warrior* episode, when Dr. Kelsey was captured by the Grumblions and sent to somewhere else. You know, when her evil twin, Krista, took her place and almost married Captain Stone. I mean I really think there's a portal next to my desk and things just fall in. In fact, I bet there's some little space alien kid somewhere who keeps trying to figure out why she has two boxes of crayons and three bottles of glue and . . ."

"Nice try, kiddo," Mom cut me off, unimpressed, "but this is coming out of your savings account."

"Okay," I said, sighing, "I'll try harder." Suddenly, I had a great thought. "Hey, Mom!" I said excitedly, "If my paper wins, will you come to the assembly and watch me on stage with Dr. Kelsey?"

"Well," Mom said, "that would be nice. But, honey, just do the best you can. You know only one child can have the highest grade. I'll be very proud of you if you just try hard and do a good job on your report."

Something about the tone of her voice bugged me. I knew what she really meant.

"You don't think I can do it, do you?" I was hurt.

"Of course you can, Paige. If you want to. I just want you to know that I'm proud of you whether you have the best grade or not." She reached for the iced tea to pour herself another glass.

I was sure then: She didn't think I could do it. I was going to say something about how could a kid believe in herself when her own mother didn't believe in her. But I didn't get a chance because, just then, I heard the familiar strains of the *Star Warrior* theme music coming from the television set in the living room.

"Can I be excused, Mom, please, please?" I jumped up. *"Star Warrior* is on."

"Wait a minute," she said. "Have you finished your homework?"

"I think so. All I had to do was to study for the spelling test tomorrow and finish some math worksheets."

"What about your paper?" asked Mom. "You didn't mention that."

"Oh, I don't have to start that yet, Mom. I have three whole weeks." I spoke impatiently. I could hear the theme music winding down as the show started.

"You know, honey, that time will go by very quickly," Mom said.

"Don't worry, Mom. There's nothing I can do tonight, anyway. We don't even go to the library to do research until tomorrow."

"Okay," said Mom. "Go ahead. It's *your* paper."

I had this sinking feeling in my stomach when she said that, but I ignored it. After all, I still had plenty of time.

We cruised through the darkest reaches of the farthest galaxy. I, Dr. Kelsey Strongheart, stood at the helm of the star cruiser. Captain Stone Griffith's handsome face appeared in the communicatron window. He looked worried.

"It's a dangerous mission, Kelsey," he said gravely. "Are you sure you're ready for it?"

"Of course, Stone, darling." I tossed my stylish wavy hair away from my face and studied my two-inch, candy-apple red fingernails. "Don't worry, Precious. I'll rescue the little Nimbians and be back at the Starship in time for my manicure."

"Of course you will, Honeybunch!" Captain Stone looked relieved.

"Oh, by the way," I said, strolling over to pick up my virtual crysto-laser, "I have a little stop to make on the way back."

"Where are you off to, Snookums?" asked Stone.

"I'm going to be stopping on Earth, which is the third planet from the star they call the Sun, in the Milky Way galaxy. I've promised to judge a little contest at an elementary school there. In fact," I paused, pleased with myself, "I've decided to give my very own crysto-laser to one worthy child."

"You are as kind as you are beautiful, my sweet!" Stone's face loomed large in the communicatron window.

"Indeed," I smiled at him. "I've also decided that, just maybe, if this child should prove worthy enough, I might bring her back here. What do you think of that, dear? Would you like a little child of our own?"

Stone looked lovingly at me and opened his mouth to reply. "Woof! Woof! Woof! Ah-wooooo!"

"Stone, darling? Is something wrong?" I darted to the communicatron and began to push buttons and spin dials. What was going on?

"Woof! Woof! Woof!"

Wait a minute! That noise is so familiar, I thought, puzzled. The star cruiser mysteriously began fading away. Captain Stone sounded just like . . . . Peevers.

In fact, it was Peevers, barking her head off. I pushed my tangled curls out of my eyes and squinted at the morning light streaming through the curtains. Rolling

38

over, I pulled my pillow over my head. "Shut up, Peevers . . . you annoying mutt," I muttered into the pillow. "I've never met a dog more in need of obedience school."

"School! . . . Oh, no!" I bolted to a sitting position and stared at the digital Sailor Moon alarm clock on the night stand. "9:00 A.M.," the red numbers flashed relentlessly. I had forgotten to set the alarm. "I'm going to be late again!" I yelled, throwing back the covers and hopping out of bed. I had been oversleeping a lot lately.

"Mark! Mark! Wake up!" I said, shaking my little brother.

"I'm tired," he mumbled, rolling over and kicking the covers. Green plastic soldiers from last night's battle tumbled to the floor.

"Hurry up, cat turd! We're late," I said, searching for yesterday's clothes to throw on.

"Okay, space cadet!" Mark shot back.

I decided to let his "space cadet" insult go by, for the time being. Instead, I rushed to Mom's room to wake her up. But her bed was empty.

"We'll save you money!!!" an announcer's voice sang from the television in the living room. Following the sound, I found Mom curled up on the sofa, asleep. She was still wearing her blue sleeveless top and white shorts from yesterday. Her brown hair was spread across her face and she was cuddling the remote control from the television like a teddy bear.

"Mom! Wake up. We missed the bus. We're late." I shook her shoulder.

"Oh my goodness! What time is it?" Mom sat up quickly. "I guess I'll have to drive you to school."

"Mo-om," Mark came in, dressed only in his Spider Man underpants. His curly brown hair was standing up on his head like he had stuck his finger in an electric outlet. "There are no shirts in my shirt drawer and no pants in my pants drawer! What should I do?"

"Look in the dirty clothes basket," said Mom, rubbing her eyes and squinting at him. "Pick the cleanest things you can find! What have I done with my glasses?" Mom patted the sofa around her and searched down between the cushions.

"I'm hungry!" Mark's words trailed off as he left the room in search of school clothes.

"Can we have Pop Tarts in the car on the way to school?" I asked, hopefully. Mrs. Barnett says Pop Tarts are junk food, and she won't let Breanna eat them. But I like them, especially the kind with frosting and sprinkles.

"I guess so," said Mom. "I wish I had time to make you

a good breakfast," she sighed. Pointing to the coffee table, she squinted and asked, "Are my glasses there?"

I reached over to pick up the glasses, then stopped. Wow! They were laying on top of the newspaper's classified advertising section, where Mom had circled lots of ads with pink, orange and yellow markers. Condensation from a glass of water set on top of the ads had caused the ink to run together in a halo, staining the paper.

How beautiful! It was a sunset. No, it was the corona of a brand new star. Dad taught me that word, "corona," when he took me and Mark to Bracato's for Italian ice cream on one of our weekend visits. I remember that I was talking so much that my ice cream melted and dripped on the tile floor. Dad bought me another one.

That's it! Maybe it could be *melting* spumoni ice cream. No, wait. I think spumoni has green in it. Or is that Neapolitan ice cream? I couldn't remember. It looked so pretty reflected through the water in the glass. Hey! I had an idea. What if I spilled the water just a little . . .

Thinking about the glorious way the colors would fan out, I reached down for the glass, starting to tip it.

"Paige, be careful! You're going to spill that." Mom's voice interrupted my thoughts sharply. "Hand me my glasses, *please.*"

"Sorry," I said, righting the glass and grabbing her glasses. Maybe later, I thought, glancing back at the colorful newspaper, regretfully. But then again, maybe not. If I made too much of a mess, I'd have to explain what I was thinking.

Instead, I asked, "Did you find any good jobs yet, Mom?"

"No, honey, not yet," she said, stretching and yawning. "Actually, I've been starting to think about the possibilities of opening my own business."

"What kind of business?" I asked.

"I don't know yet. I'm just thinking about it. Goodness, why on earth is that dog barking?"

"Mom, look!" Mark cried. "Peevers stole Mousie!" Mark drew in his breath in amazement. "Wow! Look at Fishbreath! That cat's crazy!"

Fishbreath was Kelly LeBlanc's big orange cat. The LeBlancs were our next-door neighbors, and Mousie was Fishbreath's beloved rubber toy.

Though Peevers barked frantically, Fishbreath was not afraid of her or, for that matter, any dog. Right then, Fishbreath had Peevers cornered in our garage. Mousie lay captive in the corner behind Peevers. Fishbreath was pacing like an angry tiger, hissing and spitting, demanding

Mousie. Peevers jumped up and down excitedly, barking and howling, eyes searching from side to side for a way around Fishbreath. But the big cat was not about to let Peevers escape.

"Oh, Peevers! You naughty dog!" Mom laughed. "You picked the wrong victim this time!" Mom rescued Mousie and gave her to Fishbreath, who strutted off with her toy in her mouth, tail twitching victoriously. Peevers' tail, on the other hand, was drooping between her legs. She halfheartedly followed our car down the driveway as we hurried toward school.

As the car pulled on to Milton Street, Mark asked, "Mom, is it a Jeanne Q. Learner day?" For some reason, Mark always called his doctor by her full name, which he liked. Dr. Learner, in turn, called him, "Marcus C. Bradley." Surprisingly, the "C" is for "Christopher" not "cat turd."

"No, Mark. Not today. Today is Tuesday. You visit Dr. Learner on Thursdays," said Mom.

"Why do you like going there?" I asked. "You don't do anything there but play."

"She has cool toys, and she really likes me."

"Mom, I don't think it does him any good," I said. "Mark is still psycho." I made a face at my brother. "Besides, Dad says she's not a real doctor, that she just likes to take our money. So why do you bother to send Mark to see her?"

"I am not psycho!" Mark yelled, punching me in the arm. "I'm tense and deaf to orders. Tell her, Mom!"

Mom started to laugh, then stopped. "I'm sorry, Mark. I didn't mean to laugh. It's not 'tense and deaf to orders,' it's 'attention deficit disorder.' But, don't worry about remembering all of that. You can just call it 'ADD.' And it's definitely not the same as being crazy!"

Pausing a moment to round a corner, she continued, "Paige, I don't want to hear you call Mark 'psycho' again! ADD just means that Mark has a chemical imbalance in his brain that makes it hard for him to control himself and to pay attention consistently."

"I don't know about that," I said. "Didn't Dad say that ADD is just an excuse and that all Mark really needs is a 'good paddling' once in a while?"

"Oh, nonsense!" said Mom, sounding very annoyed. "If that were true, then your dad wouldn't have turned out the way he did! Your Grandma certainly spanked him enough, and he's still operating in hyperdrive! Insensitive and selfish and likely to start trouble just because he's bored! If he didn't make so much money, he would never be able to get people to put up with him!"

I felt funny in my stomach. "Mom, I don't like it when you say bad things about my daddy."

Mom looked sorry. "Oh, gosh! I know that, and I'm sorry, honey! I don't know what gets into me."

"Anyway, I'd rather be hyper than a space cadet like you!" said Mark.

"Yeah, well, you're not only a hyper cat turd, you're a . . . . a. . . . hairy cockroach!" I retorted.

"Space cadet! Space cadet!" sang Mark.

Before I could say anything, Mom interrupted in her sternest voice, "That's enough, you two! I don't want to hear any more name-calling. Now grab your backpacks and lunch boxes. We're at school."

I glared at Mark as Mom's station wagon pulled up to the front of the school. Probst Elementary is an old brick school that looks like a haunted castle with towers on the corners. I figured I'd tell the cat turd off on the way up the old stone steps into school, out of Mom's earshot. Mark bounced out of the car, and I followed quickly.

But I didn't get far. "Paige, you forgot to close the car door!" Mom called. I hurried back. Just before I slammed it, she said, "By the way, I put your new crayons in your backpack. Take good care of them."

By that time, Mark had already gone off to his

kindergarten class. Mr. Hubble, his teacher, did not require tardy slips if you were late. Mrs. Bourgeois, however, insisted on them for the fourth graders. So I had to face Mrs. Landry.

5
Late for Take-off

Mrs. Landry was the worst part of being late. She had a way of looking at you that made you feel like you just let out a huge burp in the school library in front of your whole class. The rumor was that she was so fat because she ate kids who got sent to the office more than three times. I, of course, didn't believe that (at least not since first grade).

I walked as quietly as I could up to Mrs. Landry's desk, trying to decide if I should make up an excuse. ("I'm sorry, Mrs. Landry, the limo driver didn't show up. You just can't get good help these days!" or "Gosh, Mrs. Landry, my mom had to stop and rescue a homeless man who jumped off a bridge and, well, by the time the local TV reporters were through interviewing her, the time had just slipped by!")

Before I could say anything, however, Mrs. Landry looked up from her work and sighed heavily. Sure enough, she gave me that look. I decided nothing would help.

"Paige Bradley! Late again." Mrs. Landry shook her

head and thrust a scribbled pink sheet of paper at me. "If you continue to be late, Paige, Mrs. Martin is going to have to call your mother."

"Yes ma'am," I said quickly, snatching the tardy slip and stuffing it in my pocket.

Taking a deep breath in the hallway, I tried to open the door to Mrs. Bourgeois' room as quietly as I could. I absolutely hated the first few moments of entering the classroom late. As usual, the classroom hum ceased for a moment as kids looked up from their work, almost hopefully, to see who was coming in. Just me, late as usual. The noise resumed.

I approached Mrs. Bourgeois' desk.

"Good morning, Paige," she said crisply. "You've already missed our trip to the library and half of this period's class, which is art. I'm sorry that you didn't make it to the library because everyone else checked out books to do research for their papers. You'll have to find some other way to do your research." Mrs. Bourgeois did not sound like she felt sorry for me. She sounded annoyed. "Oh, by the way, did you bring last week's library book to return? I'll take it."

"No, ma'am," I said. "I don't have it." It was a Goosebumps book. I think it was called *The Bloody*

Vampire Wolf from the Haunted Castle on Terror Marsh, or something like that. I didn't even get to read it because I lost it at school the same day I checked it out.

Mrs. Bourgeois shook her head. "Well, you know you're not allowed to check out new library books until you have returned the old ones."

I didn't say anything; I just looked at my sneakers.

"Well, here are some color-by-number pages on the planets. Go to your desk and get to work." I exchanged the crumpled tardy slip from my pocket for the work. Mrs. Bourgeois went back to writing something in the big black grade book on her desk.

Standing there, I felt sad, wishing my teacher would smile or act happy to see me. I remembered Mr. Rodriguez saying that Mrs. Bourgeois liked me and wanted to help me. It would be silly, but I wanted to ask her if it was true. That would have sounded so corny that I just couldn't bring myself to ask. So instead, I just stood there, uncertainly, watching the top of her head.

The top of Mrs. Bourgeois' head, particularly her hair, was one of my favorite things about her. I had always been fascinated by it. It was molded around her head like stiff, silver cotton candy and covered with mesmerizing swirl patterns. I suddenly had a funny vision of her, totally bald, sticking her head in one of those cotton candy machines every morning.

I studied her hair. Up close, it didn't look much like cotton candy at all. But it did look very stiff and sticky like it was coated with spun sugar or something. One of the most unusual things about her hair was that it never moved. I always watched it carefully on windy days when Mrs. Bourgeois had playground duty. Not once had I ever see a single hair stir.

The swirls reminded me of a Christmas card we got last Christmas from my Aunt Marie. It showed an ice-covered pond full of graceful skaters in old-fashioned clothes. They twirled about on the ice, and you could see the marks left by their skates. I thought about Aunt Marie, who is one of my favorite aunts. Last Christmas, she took me to see a real ballet called *The Nutcracker*.

And then, out of nowhere, the perfect phrase popped into my mind: "Sugar plum fairies danced on her head!" That was it! Perfect! The swirl patterns were left by the graceful dancers' feet of Sugar Plum fairies. I imagined Mrs. Bourgeois sleeping. As she dreamed, sparkling clouds of fairies danced, spun and flitted around her head, like dizzy fireflies.

Unexpectedly, my teacher looked up. The fairies

vanished. She seemed surprised to see me still standing there in the same spot.

"Did you need something? . . . If not, go to your seat. You've already missed the first part of the school day." Mrs. Bourgeois did not wait for an answer. She pushed her chair back and stood up to erase something on the board.

I walked slowly to my desk, sat down, and put my books away.

Jessica said in a too-loud whisper, "Paige Bradley, why are you always late?" I knew that Jessica didn't care why I was late. Her question was meant for Pauline to hear. I turned to look at them. They had finished their color-by-number pages early and had nothing else to do.

Jessica was twirling one end of her long blond hair around her finger. "I checked four books out of the library on my subject, and even took some notes. My mom showed me how. See?"

I looked at her neat handwriting, two pages of it. On the first sheet she had written the title and author of a book, and had page numbers in the margins. When I handed it back to her without a word, she said, "My paper is going to be really good. How are you going to do yours without any research?"

My heart felt very heavy because I couldn't even imagine myself taking notes like that. But I couldn't give Jessica the satisfaction of knowing that. So I replied, "I've got plenty of research already."

"What are you talking about?" said Jessica. "How could you have done your research already? We only got the assignment yesterday."

"I certainly did," I said, making it up as I went along. "I wrote to NASA. In fact, I wrote to Sally Ride when we were studying astronauts. She sent me a bunch of really good stuff that I'm going to use in my paper." That wasn't true, but it sounded good.

It must have impressed Jessica and Pauline, for they actually fell silent for a minute. I could see on their faces

that I had surprised them. In fact, they looked worried!

"Oh, well. Don't worry, Jessica," said Pauline finally. "Even if she did get stuff from Sally Ride, it doesn't matter. She's so spacey that she'll forget her paper on the day it's due. She's no threat to either of us. And we've already agreed: whichever one of us gets the prize from Dr. Kelsey, we'll let the other one borrow it three days a week!" They gave each other a special, best-friends smile that made me feel as if I were all alone in the world.

"You're right," said Jessica. "Paige can't possibly win. Even if she does hand it in, her handwriting will be so bad that Mrs. Bourgeois won't be able to read it."

"Oh, just shut up!" I said, turning around quickly. Even though I couldn't see them any longer, I could still hear their mocking giggles from behind me.

6
Collision Course

It's amazing how quickly the first week of that competition rocketed by. Breanna and I spent a lot of time discussing how exciting it would be to sit on the stage with Dr. Kelsey, right in front of the whole school. We also talked a couple of times about dropping in on Mr. Rodriguez, but we never did. All in all, it was a pretty good week, up until Friday.

From the very first moment in school, however, Friday felt like a mission that was doomed. First of all, I had to face Mrs. Landry for being late again. Then, when it was time for the class to check our spelling homework, I realized I had left my workbook at home.

"Paige, I can't believe you forgot your spelling workbook again!" Mrs. Bourgeois said in front of the whole class. She sighed loudly. "I'm afraid I am going to have to give you an unsatisfactory mark."

I winced. That was bad enough, but things soon got even worse.

"You'll have to slide your chair next to Keith and look on with him," Mrs. Bourgeois said with another sigh. Look on with Keith! Was she trying to be funny? I wanted to die. I hated sitting next to any boy, but Keith Guidry was definitely the *worst*.

Jessica and Pauline giggled at my punishment, but Mrs. Bourgeois took no notice of them. Breanna glanced back at me with eyes that seemed to say, "Be brave, Paige. We'll decontaminate you at recess."

I waited as long as I could before pushing my chair towards Keith's desk, barely close enough to see his workbook. I stared stonily at its dog-eared right page, which was covered with his messy scrawl. My cheeks burned as I felt the eyes of the other kids on me. Keith, however, seemed to think it was funny. He began to burp softly in my direction, just out of the range of Mrs. Bourgeois' hearing aid. The other kids giggled. I wanted the ground to open up and swallow me.

The rest of the day didn't go any better.

I had no one to eat with at lunch because Breanna's mom picked her up for a doctor's appointment. At recess, I fell and skinned my knee on the asphalt playground trying to jump doubles, which I was never any good at.

During math, which is my worst subject, it was my

turn to write problems on the board. All but two of my answers were wrong, and everybody laughed. When I got back to my desk, Jessica started to say something in a loud whisper. I just knew it was going to be something like "Hey, spacey! Why are you so dumb in math?"

I couldn't help it. Without thinking, I turned around and yelled, "Shut up!" So Mrs. Bourgeois made me write forty lines: "I will not disrupt the class."

"I was only trying to tell Paige that she has chalk dust all over her back," said Jessica in a too-sweet voice.

Before I could finish writing my lines, Mrs. Bourgeois asked us to turn in our outlines for our research papers, then went up and down the aisles collecting them. I slid down in my seat, hoping she'd forget to stop at my desk. No such luck.

"Paige, your outline, please." Mrs. Bourgeois stood next to my desk, waiting.

"I don't have one," I replied in a small voice.

"Please see me after school, Paige," she said sternly, moving on to Breanna. My friend handed in her outline quickly and then turned around as the teacher moved on. "Where's yours?" my friend whispered, her brown eyes wide.

"I didn't do it yet," I said. "I don't even have my books.

I missed going to the library, remember?"

"What are you going to do?" she asked.

"I'll write it next week," I said with more confidence than I felt. "Besides we have three whole weeks to finish the paper."

"Well, not really," whispered Breanna. "We only have two weeks left now."

"Oh, yeah. I guess you're right," I said. "Well, two weeks is still a long way off."

Things can't get any worse than this, I thought; but I was wrong. At the end of the last period of the day, when I was packing my books, something fell out of my backpack, and Keith picked it up. He started to plunk it on my desk, then stopped, eyeing me fiendishly as he examined my new crayons.

"Hey!" he hooted. "Paige has Barney crayons!" He was referring, of course, to that stupid purple dinosaur from television.

I lunged for the crayons just after he waved them above his head for everyone to see. I groaned. Didn't Mom know that no self-respecting fourth grader would be caught dead with anything with Barney on it? How could she do this to me? And why couldn't that portal to the alternate universe open up and swallow me *now?*

"Give 'em back!" I hissed fiercely at Keith, trying to keep my voice low. Something in my face must have scared him a little because he dropped them for a moment. Then, with something even more devilish in mind, he reached to take them up again—just as I reached over to grab them, too. Crack! Our heads connected, hard.

"Ouch!" I yelled, forgetting to be quiet.

"Watch out you don't catch Keith's head lice, Paige!" said Pauline. Everyone around me snickered.

Mrs. Bourgeois laid her hand on my shoulder, pulling me up.

"Paige and Keith! I am ashamed of you! Sit down at your desks, both of you, right now." We did as she said, glaring at each other. Mrs. Bourgeois held the crayons up.

"Now, who do these belong to?" she asked.

"They're hers," said Keith, sullenly.

"Oh, no they're not." I yelled, suddenly inspired. "They're his!" I knew I shouldn't lie, but Keith deserved it. He had been trying to embarrass me.

"Mine?" Keith yelped. "No way! They're hers! Mrs. Bourgeois, you gotta believe me."

Mrs. Bourgeois looked at me. "They're definitely his!" I said again.

Mrs. Bourgeois looked confused. "Well, they're mine now," she said after a minute and returned to her desk, crayons in hand. Good! She can keep them, I thought. Then I remembered my mom's warning to take good care of my supplies, and realized I was about to sacrifice more of my savings.

Finally, when the last bell rang to dismiss the other kids, I walked slowly up to Mrs. Bourgeois' desk, trailing my backpack. "You wanted to see me after school, ma'am?"

She glanced up from grading papers and folded her hands in front of her. "Well, Paige," she said finally, "what happened to your outline?"

"I guess . . . . I mean, I just, um, didn't do one yet," I said, avoiding her eyes. "I missed going to the library and haven't been able to do my research yet."

"You know," Mrs. Bourgeois said in slow, measured tones, "the outline is a very important part of this assignment. It counts toward your grade. I'll have to subtract points because it's late."

"Subtract points!" I said. "Why? I don't really need to do an outline. I can just write the paper."

"No," said Mrs. Bourgeois. "An outline is definitely required. I want to make sure you're headed in the right direction. I don't want you to waste your time if you misunderstand your assignment. In addition, I believe that an outline is an essential part of planning and organizing a good paper. You'll just have to bring yours next week. You may leave to catch your bus now." She picked up her pen and resumed grading papers.

My heart felt heavy as I headed home. Subtracting points because of missing a stupid outline wasn't fair. After all, outline or no outline, I was going to do the best research paper, so I deserved the best grade. But because of Mrs. Bourgeois' dumb rule about outlines, I began to worry about my chances of meeting Dr. Kelsey.

7

Through the Branches to the Stars

I hardly ate my dinner that night. Afterward, I called Breanna to talk about what jerks Jessica and Pauline were. That would help me feel better, I thought.

"Oh, hi, Paige!" she said, answering the phone. "I'm kind of busy right now. Can I call you back later?"

"Busy? Doing what?"

"Well, my mom is helping me download some pictures of Pluto from the Internet. You should see them! They're great. I'm going to use them for my paper."

"Why are you doing homework on Friday night? Isn't that carrying things a bit too far?"

"Not this time," she said. "My mom is helping me. After all, it's not every day you get a chance to meet Dr. Kelsey. I'll call you back tomorrow."

"Yeah . . . . sure. I guess," I said, hanging up. Now I felt worse than before. Maybe I should be working on my paper, too. But how to start? I had no books and no ideas.

I walked into my bedroom, flopped on the bed belly first, and lay there thinking. It was hot and stuffy, and I could hear Mark playing with Peevers in the back yard.

Ouch! I felt a tiny pinprick on my arm. I sat up quickly, smacking the spot. Pulling away my hand, I saw the dead body of a smushed mosquito, resting in a droplet of my own blood. How had that miserable bug gotten in the house? Looking up, I saw that my bedroom window was open and the screen had fallen out. Silhouetted against the peach-colored sunset, my tree looked cool and calm.

That gave me an idea. I climbed out over the windowsill and dropped down into the front yard. I padded through the soft grass toward the comfort of my tree. Grabbing the two lowest branches, I pulled myself up and climbed to the highest branch where I could sit safely. With my arms wrapped around the thinning tree trunk and my cheek resting against the rough bark, I felt better.

To my tree I whispered, "You know that paper I'm writing so I can meet Dr. Kelsey . . . ?" Soon I was confiding all the moments of the rotten, rotten day I had. By now the sun had dipped below the horizon, and the warm glow of the sky was shot with cool blues in a display that was much too pretty to spoil with tales of a disastrous day. So I just sat in unhappy silence, hugging the tree.

A few tears blurred my vision of the branches and sunset, but they couldn't block out my thoughts of the assembly that I was dreading. There was Dr. Kelsey, in her *Star Warrior* uniform, reaching down to shake hands with .... Jessica Patino. Jessica was saying, "Well, if you *insist* on giving me your crysto-laser, you can. But I already have three of those. Of course, it would look nice with the rest of my collection."

I knew then that I was not about to let that happen! I really had to win. After all, there were still two weeks left before the assembly—fourteen more days to do a really good job on my paper. I'm no quitter, I thought. It doesn't matter if nobody else believes I can do it. I'll do such a good job that I'll earn their respect. I'll show them!

"I *can* do this!" I said out loud. "I can't change the fact that Mrs. Bourgeois is going to take off points because my outline is late. But I do have two more weeks. This calls for something really special to impress Mrs. Bourgeois." The mosquitoes, who also never quit, had gotten just about as bad as I could stand. I climbed down, puzzling over what I could do to impress Mrs. Bourgeois.

Leaning against my tree, I found the inspiration I needed. I know! I won't just write a paper, I'll do something even better. But what? I bet I could get extra points if I skip the silly illustrations and make real stars instead! Three-dimensional illustrations, big, bright sparkly stars that Mrs. Bourgeois will have to give me an "A" for. Not with real fire, though—I'd probably get in trouble for that. But Christmas tree lights would be just the thing! However I did it, it would be so wonderful that Mrs. Bourgeois would forgive me for not doing an outline after all.

After making sure that Mom wasn't looking outside, I skipped over to my bedroom window and boosted myself over the ledge. I decided to go to bed and get an early start on my illustrations the next day. Having a plan made me feel so good that I could nearly stand the mosquitoes that had come in while I'd been outside. Just in case, though, I closed the window and got the bug spray.

☆ ☆ ☆

My new determination brought immediate results. The next morning as I ate breakfast, I handed Mom a list of the things I needed.

"Five boxes of tin foil, large Styrofoam balls, Christmas tree lights, gold and silver paint, twine, shiny foil wrapping paper, flashlights, clear glass marbles, sequins, a gallon of gold glitter . . . ." Mom started reading out loud, then paused. "Paige, what do you want all of this stuff for?"

"It's for my star project, Mom," I said, biting into a warm biscuit.

"Yes, but I'm not convinced that you need all of this . . . Are you sure you need a whole gallon of glitter?" Mom's eyes strayed to the living room rug, probably envisioning it covered with glitter.

"Yeah, I'm sure," I said with my mouth full.

"I thought you were supposed to do a written report," she said, still studying the list.

"I am. But I'm supposed to have illustrations, too, and I want to make mine really special. They're going to be three-dimensional! They'll be so awesome that Mrs. Bourgeois will *have* to give me a good grade."

"Well, okay," she said, hesitantly, "if you're sure you need these things. We have to run some errands today, anyway, so we'll pick them up."

"Thanks," I said, pouring my juice.

"One thing, though," Mom added. "Whatever it is you're making, I'd like you to make it in the garage. Not in the house!"

"No problem," I said, swallowing a big gulp of breakfast. Pushing my chair away from the table, I began humming the *Star Warrior* theme song softly under my breath. I was making great progress now. Or so I thought.

8
Technical Difficulties

Working on my stars kept me very busy that weekend. Mom made Mark promise to stay out of the garage until I finished. But on Monday night I took a break from them because Breanna came over to play. Not wanting her to see what I was working on, I kept quiet about my super secret surprise in the garage. We just watched *Star Warrior* together after dinner and then acted out the story outside while we waited for her mom to come get her. Through the darkness, the moon and stars shone in the sky.

"Did you know," said Breanna, pointing upward, "that the planet Pluto is not always the ninth planet from the sun? Sometimes it's the eighth planet, depending on where Neptune is. What's really weird, though, is that Pluto is even smaller than our moon!"

"Really? Can you see it up there?" I asked.

"Nah, it's way too far," she said. "It has its very own moon, though. It's called Charon. Its moon is so big that it's almost like another planet. Isn't that interesting?"

"Yeah, I guess so," I said. I could tell she was pretty excited about knowing that stuff.

"How is your outline coming?" she asked.

"Oh, my paper is going great," I said excitedly, remembering my work in the garage.

"Really! I'm so glad," said Breanna. She honestly did look relieved. "I hope one of us has the highest grade. After all, it would be pretty awful if somebody like Jessica or Pauline won. They'd never stop bragging about it!"

"Yeah. If they get any more stuck up, they'll have to be scraped off the ceiling."

We both laughed.

"Anyway, try to be on time tomorrow," said Breanna, dusting herself off as her mom's car pulled into the driveway. "And don't forget it's library day."

Breanna didn't really have to remind me. I caught the bus and arrived at school right on time the next morning! Once inside the classroom, I looked at the clock and counted the minutes till I could go to the library to get my books on stars. Unfortunately, Mrs. Bourgeois announced that we wouldn't be going to the library first period after all. We had to switch with Mrs. Evans' class and were going last period instead. Oh, well, I could wait. I felt just great about my paper whenever I thought about the special surprise I was creating in the garage at home.

Sometimes when you feel good, you can do a lot of things right. So it was with me: That Tuesday started out pretty well. In art class I made a pretty collage for Breanna because her birthday was the next day. We were supposed to use clippings from old magazines to make a picture, but I decided to make a card for Breanna instead. I had the idea of adding some dried wildflowers I had pressed in my spelling book. I also found some old candies in my pencil box and glued those on, too. It may sound dumb, but it came out pretty. In fact, Mrs. Bourgeois saw it and told me she liked it. Even smelly Keith came over to my desk to admire it.

"This is very creative, Paige," Mrs. Bourgeois said. "If you'll put it on my desk, I'll hang it up for the class to see."

"Thanks, anyway," I whispered, "but this is for Breanna." I felt warm inside, confident that I could do pretty good work in art.

After lunch, Mrs. Bourgeois gave us a surprise social studies quiz. I worked hard on writing my answers neatly. I don't usually have to study for social studies because it's easy for me. Mrs. Bourgeois actually called me up to her desk afterwards and complimented me on my handwriting.

"Paige, this is wonderful," she said. "You bumped the

69

lines, and you left spaces between your words. I can read this!" She sounded surprised. I beamed back at her. "See, Paige, you *can* do it when you try!"

Yup! If the day had ended right there, it would have been perfect. But do I have that kind of luck? Well, you know the answer.

"Now, boys and girls," Mrs. Bourgeois said near the end of the day, "get out the library books that you will be returning today and line up by the door. One line of boys and one line of girls, please," she said, pushing her chair back and standing up.

On my way to the door, I stopped in my tracks when all of Mrs. Bourgeois' words finally registered in my brain. That part about "the library books that you will be returning today" caused my heart to sink and my knees to feel weak. I rushed back to my desk, pulling books and papers out of it, spilling them on the floor. Oh no! Where was it?

Everyone had lined up by the door now. Mrs. Bourgeois noticed me furiously shuffling through the pile of papers at my desk.

"Paige," she asked, "are you ready?"

"The Bloody Vampire Wolf from the Haunted Castle on Terror Marsh!" I gasped.

"What?" Mrs. Bourgeois asked, cupping a hand behind her ear as if she didn't trust her hearing aid.

"*The Bloody Vampire Wolf from the Haunted Castle on Terror Marsh!* I can't find it," I replied, frantically.

"Her library book," explained Carol. "She can't find her library book."

"Oh, is that all." Mrs. Bourgeois looked annoyed. "Well, then you'll just have to return it later or pay the fine. In any event, you won't be able to check out any books today. You know the rule."

Ignoring her, I knelt over the pile on the floor, turning over loose papers and pushing my books around. I had to find that book!

"Paige, we can't wait all day for you, and I can't leave you here. You'll just have to come with us to the library. You may look at a magazine while the rest of the class selects their books." Mrs. Bourgeois tapped her foot impatiently. "Come along now, Paige." Her voice was insistent now.

I shoved the contents of my desk into a loose pile and pushed it underneath my desk, then rose slowly and dragged myself to the end of the line. I heard whispering. The other kids knew that without any research materials my paper was doomed, utterly and hopelessly impossible.

Tears sprang to my eyes. I stared at my feet.

"Paige." Mrs. Bourgeois noticed the pile under my desk. "You can't leave that mess on the floor."

I looked back; it did look pretty bad.

"You'll have to stay behind and pick that up." She seemed exasperated. "Now hurry up and meet us in the library. Don't dawdle." Shaking her head, she followed the last kid out of the room.

I stuffed great handfuls of paper and other books back into my desk and then, although Mrs. Bourgeois had warned me not to dawdle, took my time making my way to the library. After all, it didn't truly matter if I got there quickly. It wasn't like they were going to let me check anything out.

Squeak. Squeak. Squeak. In the quiet corridor, the noise of my sneakers on the tile floor echoed too loudly for my comfort. I always felt a guilty pleasure at being alone in the empty halls while classes were in session. For children who did venture out on their own, silence was required as surely as in any church. Over the noise of my sneakers, I could barely hear the muffled voices of teachers from behind the closed doors of classrooms.

As if looking into a giant doll house with a missing wall, I could see in my imagination all those kids in all

72

those classrooms—from the littlest preschoolers who were napping to the great big fifth graders on the second floor, concentrating intently, silently on their work. I alone moved, noisy and free.

I was so intent on my thoughts that I didn't notice Mr. Rodriguez standing inside the open door of the lost-and-found closet. His friendly greeting—"Hi, Paige! How's it going?"—broke the silence so suddenly that my heart leaped as if Grumblions had attacked out of nowhere.

Spinning around quickly, I caught the sole of my sneakers on the tile and stumbled. "I'm going to the library," I said, righting myself. The last thing I wanted to do was to tell him how my paper was going.

He looked at me as if he were expecting a real answer to his question. To distract him, I nodded to the lost-and-found closet and asked, "Did you lose something?"

"No," said Mr. Rodriguez, "I was just straightening up a bit in here." Looking carefully at me, he repeated, "I mean it—are you doing okay?"

"Fine," I said, avoiding his eyes.

"So," he persisted, "your paper is going well?"

"Not really," I admitted, finally. "I'm kind of in trouble, as usual."

"Why? What happened?"

"Nothing. Forget it." Why wouldn't this guy leave me alone? Couldn't he just let me fail without rubbing my nose in it?

"I know," he said cheerfully. "You want me to guess. Okay, I know what you did. You're the kid who climbed up the school flagpole and dropped a water balloon on Mrs. Martin's head. Was that you?"

"No." I smiled a little, despite myself.

"Oh, wait a minute. I know," Mr. Rodriguez pointed at me. "You must be the kid who painted a mustache on the picture of Miss Probst in the school library! Did you do that?"

"No, of course not!" I giggled.

"Well, then," said Mr. Rodriguez, "I give up. I guess you'll just have to tell me yourself."

"Well," I said, "I'm behind on the actual writing part of my paper. And now I won't even be able to start for another week!"

Tears pooled in the corners of my eyes, and my nose started to run. I told him about missing library day twice and not having any research materials. By the time I had finished, tears were running down my cheeks.

I wiped my nose on the back of my hand and sniffled, "You know, seeing Dr. Kelsey from the back of the auditorium is probably going to be no better than seeing her on television. And knowing I had a chance to actually meet her and blew it, well, that's just about the worst thing I can think of." I was blubbering now. Good thing nobody else was around.

"Hang on a minute," said Mr. Rodriguez. "I know you think all is lost, but don't surrender this battle yet."

He put a hand on my shoulder and gently pointed me towards the lost-and-found closet. "Now come on. Stop crying. Dr. Kelsey wouldn't give up, and I don't think you want to, either. She'd probably just try something different."

I looked up at him through my tears. "Yeah, I know," I said. "I guess she'd probably turn on the duplicatron and make another copy of *The Bloody Vampire Wolf from the Haunted Castle on Terror Marsh.*"

"Maybe," said Mr. Rodriguez. "But, in any event, I'm at least sure that she would try to make a new plan and start over. In this case, the school duplicatron just happens to be out of order, so we have to fall back to Plan B, which is to look right here for your lost library book." He gestured towards the closet.

"Yuck," I said, hesitating. "It smells in there. Do I have to?"

"Okay, Paige," Mr. Rodriguez smiled, leaning into the

closet. "For you, I'll search through several months' worth of old, smelly discarded gym clothes and . . . . whatever this is," he said holding up a rank smelling bag that might have held some kid's snack, "to see if I can find *The Scary Monster from the Mucky Marsh.*"

"Thank you," I said, giggling as my cheeks started to dry, "but it's *The Bloody Vampire Wolf from the Haunted Castle on Terror Marsh.* It's a Goosebumps book."

"Well, there are no Goosebumps books in here at all," he said finally, straightening up and dusting off his hands. "I guess we have to move on to plan C."

"What's that?" I asked, curious now.

He closed the closet door. "Come with me a moment." Entering the main office, he said, "Mrs. Landry, please call over to the library and let Mrs. Bourgeois know that Paige Bradley is with me." Then he led me into his smaller office, closed the door, and motioned for me to sit down. I sat, watching his back, as he stood studying books on one of his high shelves.

Browsing through the titles, he said, "I have some books here that you may find useful for your paper. Some of them may be a little advanced for you, but if you're interested, and if you promise to take very good care of them, I'll let you use them."

76

"Really?" I said, suddenly feeling excited and hopeful. Then my face fell. What if I lost Mr. Rodriguez' books? Maybe he was making a mistake. I'd better warn him. "Maybe you better not loan me your books. After all, I already lost my library book."

"Well," he said. "It's a no-lose proposition for me because there's one other condition that I haven't told you about yet."

"What condition?" I asked.

"I want you to use them here. Your class goes to second recess every day at twelve-thirty for forty minutes, and I usually save that same time to catch up on my professional reading here in my office. You just come here every day for recess, and you can use my books. That way you can ask me what the hard words mean."

"You want me to give up recess?" I gasped.

"No, Paige, I don't want you to give up recess," he said quickly. "Not if you don't want to. I just told you that you could use my books if you were willing to come here at recess. It's up to you."

I slumped down in my seat to consider this carefully. Giving up recess was pretty drastic. I mean, when a teacher *made* a kid do it, that was a severe punishment. But as he said, this was my choice, and I couldn't think of a better alternative. Picturing myself shaking hands with Dr. Kelsey, I replied, "Thanks. I'll give up recess."

"Good!" said Mr. Rodriguez, getting up and opening the door for me. "I'll send a note to Mrs. Bourgeois so that she'll let you come."

When I got back to class, Breanna immediately demanded to know where I'd been. "Why did you have to go see Mr. Rodriguez? Are you in trouble?"

"Oh, he's letting me use some of his books on the stars to do my paper because I can't check out any books from the school library," I said. "I'm going to go to his office every day at second recess until I finish reading parts of those books."

"Every day!" said Breanna, "That's awful. Why didn't you just ask your mom to take you to the public library?"

Yeah, why didn't I think of that? I felt pretty dumb, losing my recesses because I had forgotten something as obvious as asking Mom to take me to the public library.

"Oh, well!" said Breanna, suddenly. "I guess you're pretty lucky, though."

"Lucky?" I asked. "What are you talking about?"

"You get to spend recess every day with Captain Stone!" she said, grinning. "Can I come sometime?"

"Oh! Yeah, sure!" Breanna thought I was lucky? I was

puzzled, but it made me feel a little better about my decision. Anyway, giving up recess would be worth it if it helped me get to meet Dr. Kelsey!

9
Against Overwhelming Odds

Since it was Tuesday, it was, as Mark would say, a "Jeanne Q. Learner Day." So after school, Mom drove us to the doctor's office. I stayed in the waiting room with Mom until Mark came out.

Dr. Learner, a short, skinny, red-haired lady, followed Mark out the door to the waiting room. "Hi, Paige," she said, smiling. "How's school?"

But I smelled a trap and muttered, "Hey," not even looking up from the magazine I was reading.

"Paige!" Mom scolded.

"Don't worry about it. Some other time." Dr. Learner waved her hand, smiling at my mom.

When we got back to our own kitchen, Mom dropped our fast food dinner and her purse and keys on the table. Mark sat down and started pulling burgers out of the bags. I was pouring a glass of milk when the doorbell rang.

"I'll get it," yelled Mark, knocking over his chair as he took off toward the front door.

"Mark, slow down!" Mom yelled. I started emptying the fast food bags, but was soon drawn to the front door by the voices of noisy, excited children.

A couple of the neighborhood kids were standing on our doorstep yelling, "Mrs. Bradley! Mrs. Bradley! Come quick!" Before I even made it outside, I knew that Peevers was in trouble again. Mom guessed, too, I thought, judging by the rolled-up newspaper in her hand. Peevers' barks reached me, though I couldn't see her.

"Okay, kids," Mom said tiredly, as if she didn't really want to know the answer to her question. "What's the matter?"

Lakesha and Kenyatta Willis, the twins from across the street, stood there along with Kelly LeBlanc. William and Elizabeth Clementson were there too, hopping up and down, excitedly.

Kelly spoke up first. "Mrs. Bradley, you have to come quick! Fishbreath is trying to drown Peevers in the Willis' pool. Hurry!"

We hurried across the street to the Willis' back yard where Mr. and Mrs. Willis stood next to their built-in swimming pool. Mr. Willis was laughing so hard that tears streamed down his face. Mrs. Willis was trying to get the attention of Fishbreath, who was circling the edge of the pool. The cat's eyes were fastened on poor Peevers, who was madly dog-paddling in the deepest part of the water, barking and howling in terror. Mousie bobbed up and down on the surface as she splashed.

"Oh, my goodness!" said Mom. "Frank, Betty, I'm very sorry!"

"I think that cat chased Peevers in there," Mrs. Willis said. "Now I can't get her to go away and let your dog come out."

Mom looked around and spied a long pole with a net hanging on the Willis' back fence. "If we can use that net over there to get Fishbreath's toy out, I'm sure she'll take it and leave," she said. And she was right. After Mom returned Mousie to Fishbreath, the cat threw Peevers a disdainful look that seemed to say, "I hope you drown," and stalked off.

"Now to get *you* out of there," said Mom to Peevers. "Here, girl! Here, girl!" It was no use. We all stood around the pool coaxing the dog, who still barked so frantically that she started swallowing water and sputtering.

"She won't drown, will she, Mom?" I fretted.

"Such a stupid dog," Mom muttered, pulling her sandals off. "A legacy from your father through and through. I guess I'll have to go in and get her myself."

"I'll do it, Mom! I'll do it!" Mark volunteered.

"No, honey, you can't swim any better than Peevers. Stay here. I *mean* it," she said, fixing a look on him that warned, "Don't even try."

"I'll go get you some towels," said Mr. Willis, heading for the house.

Mom let herself down into the pool and waded out to Peevers. The water came up only as far as her chest. As she reached for the dog's collar, Peevers closed the distance trying to lick Mom's face and slobbering all over her glasses.

"Peevers, cut it out!" Mom laughed, pulling her to the side and trying to lift the dog's slippery brown body out. But Peevers didn't make it easy. Her nails scratched madly against the side, and her tail smacked Mom's face. Suddenly a deep male voice behind us said, "Hang on! I can help."

The back of my neck turned into goosebumps. Captain Stone? It couldn't be!

But it was—almost. I turned slowly to see Mr. Rodriguez, in an old shirt and jeans, striding around the side of the house to the pool. He grabbed Peevers and hauled her out of the water, then reached down to help my mother out. Just then, Peevers, in a complete display of ingratitude, began to shake herself madly, spraying both mom and the assistant principal with water.

"Peevers! Stop it!" cried Mom. "I'm sorry!" she said to Mr. Rodriguez with an embarrassed laugh. "Thanks for your help!"

As she tried to dry her glasses on her sopping shirt, Mr. Rodriguez took them and said, "Here. I think I have a dry spot left on my shirt." He was laughing, too.

Mr. Willis came out with towels for Mom.

"Hi, Chris," he said to Mr. Rodriguez, grinning. "You should've told me you'd forgotten your swim trunks—I would've loaned you a pair."

He handed a towel to my mom, still talking to Mr. Rodriguez. "I'd offer *you* a towel, but I bet you prefer to drip dry." Mr. Rodriguez chuckled as Mr. Willis continued, "Have you met our neighbor? This is Sharon Bradley. She was just fishing her dog out of our pool." They walked around the water toward us, avoiding Peevers, who was shaking like a furry lawn sprinkler gone mad. "Sharon, this is my friend, Chris Rodriguez."

Mom reached out to shake Mr. Rodriguez hand, but stopped. "I'm sorry. I'll just get you wetter," she said, wiping her hand on the towel.

"Don't worry," said Mr. Rodriguez. He hesitated, then said, "Your name sounds so familiar."

I finally found my voice and blurted out the question uppermost in my mind. "Mr. Rodriguez! What are you doing here?"

Mr. Rodriguez noticed me for the first time. "Paige! Hi. Do you live nearby?"

"Yes. But why are you here?" I insisted.

"Paige!" Mom gave me a frown that said, "That's not very polite!"

"Oh, don't worry," said Mr. Rodriguez. "Now I know why your name is familiar. We've talked on the phone. I'm the assistant principal at Probst Elementary."

"Oh, yes," said Mom. "That's right! We sure have."

Turning to me, Mr. Rodriguez replied, "I'm here,

Paige, because Frank and I are amateur astronomers." He pointed to Mr. Willis. "We're going to be doing some stargazing tonight."

"Okay, everybody, let's go home," said Mom quickly. "I'm sorry again, Frank and Betty. If you don't mind, I'll wash these towels and bring them back tomorrow."

"See you at school, Paige," Mr. Rodriguez said.

"Come on, Peevers!" called Mom. I waved to Mr. Rodriguez as we all trooped out of the Willis' yard.

Back in our front yard, Mom decided to dry Peevers before she tracked up the house. Rubbing the dog's back, she said, "Peevers, you just never learn. But I guess I'd admire your persistence if I didn't want to kill you."

"What is 'per-sisters?'" asked Mark.

"Persistence," said Mom, "is stick-to-it-ness. It means not giving up when the going gets tough."

"Even in the face of overwhelming odds?" I asked.

"Yes," said Mom. "It means not giving up, no matter who or what you're up against."

"Do you think I have persistence, Mom?" I asked.

"Yes, Paige," said Mom, smiling. "You're very persistent when it comes to anything concerning your Dr. Kelsey. I guess she must be at the center of your entire universe!"

But for once I was serious. "Being persistent is good, isn't it?"

Mom laughed. "Most of the time," she said, as we went into the house for the evening. The next day I found out just how persistent I'd have to be.

10
Where's the Flight Plan?

"Hey," Breanna said the next day at lunch, "do you want to play with my new Vacation Fun Barbie at recess? I got her for my birthday." She took a sip from her milk carton.

"Sure," I said, pushing away that uneasy feeling I get when I know I've forgotten something.

Mrs. Barnett, Breanna's mom, showed up during lunch with a birthday cake and a plate of bright pink cookies and punch to share with the class. "Who would like to help pass out the cookies?" she asked.

I raised my hand halfheartedly, figuring Breanna's mom would select one of the other kids who were waving their arms like windmills and hollering.

But somehow Mrs. Barnett noticed me. "Paige, will you pass this plate for us?"

I jumped up quickly, then reminded myself to walk slowly and carefully with the plate of cookies. While the class was singing "Happy Birthday" to Breanna, I made sure that everyone (even Keith) got a cookie. Well, actually, Keith grabbed two cookies, but I let him get away with it.

As soon as I completed my rounds, Mrs. Bourgeois said, "Paige, it's almost time for recess. Why don't you run along to see Mr. Rodriguez?"

Everybody fell silent, looking at me. I panicked for about a second before remembering what Mrs. Bourgeois was talking about, then jumped up to leave. The class started buzzing, probably thinking I was in trouble. Embarrassed, I made a quick exit, gobbling my cookie as I went.

I hurried to Mr. Rodriguez' office where he was waiting for me by the door. He had cleared off a little table near the window. "Sit right there," he said as I came in. "Did you bring some paper to take notes?"

"No." I said, feeling stupid.

"Well, that's okay. Here's some loose leaf you can use if you decide you want to take notes. I personally find that note-taking is very helpful because then I don't have to remember all the details in my head. I can just look back at what I wrote down."

"Let's see," he said, picking up a stack of three or four books off of his desk and placing them in front of me. "This should be enough to get you started."

"They look pretty long," I said. "Are you sure these are kid books?"

"No. As a matter of fact, except for this Space Atlas here, these are not kid books," Mr. Rodriguez replied. "But I still think you can handle them.

"Besides, you won't have to read every word of them. Just read the parts that talk about what you're studying. For example, this one here is called *Cosmos*. It's by a man named Carl Sagan, and it's the book that first got me interested in astronomy. He mentions lots of things that you won't need for your paper. Nevertheless, this chapter on the life and death of stars may be very useful to you."

"Thanks," I said. "But I'll start with the kid's book, if you don't mind."

"Here it is," he said. "If you have any questions, I'll be over there reading." Soon I was so fascinated by the stars I was reading about that I forgot that Mr. Rodriguez was in the same room.

The next day, I found the Space Atlas so interesting that I finished it. I had started out taking notes, but after the first few sentences I forgot to write anything because it slowed me down too much. I doodled as I read.

On Friday (the day we were supposed to hand in our first draft), as I finished reading from the last book, I looked up to see Mr. Rodriguez leaning back in his chair staring up at his star map.

"Mr. Rodriguez," I said, following his gaze, "how come when I look at your star map, I can't see any of this stuff I'm reading about—like supernovas and black holes and binary stars? All the stars just look like little white dots to me."

"Well, that's because what you see up there is the big picture. That's what the stars would look like to the naked eye. That is, if you could see a lot more of the sky than is usually visible from earth."

"If that's what the stars look like from earth," I asked, puzzled, "then how did scientists find out about all this stuff that I'm reading in these books?"

Mr. Rodriguez sat up. I could tell he liked to talk about this. "Through the use of mathematics, good guesses, technology, and telescopes," he replied.

"Telescopes like yours?" I asked, pointing.

"Yes, in some cases, like mine, except that there are much larger telescopes in use at different observatories around the world. A telescope is a fascinating device. It adds something at the same time that it takes something else away."

"What do you mean?"

"I'll show you," he said, walking over to the window. "Look. What do you see?"

"Mrs. Alexander's pre-kindergarten class."

"Can you see all the children?"

"Yes."

"Can you see their faces? Can you tell if they're smiling or laughing?"

"Not too well," I said.

"Okay, now look through this." Mr. Rodriguez pushed the end of his telescope toward me. I stood on tiptoe and peered through it.

"Now what do you see?"

"I see a little girl . . . ." I said. "It's Elizabeth Clementson; she lives just down the street from me. She's making silly faces at somebody."

"Can you see who she's making faces at?"

"No."

"Can you tell if she's happy or sad?"

"She's pretty happy," I said. "Pretty silly, too."

"If you turn this here," Mr. Rodriguez said, adjusting a knob, "you can see Elizabeth even more clearly. You might even be able to tell what color her eyes are."

"That's called 'focusing,' isn't it?"

"Yep," said Mr. Rodriguez. "That's what I mean when

92

I say that a telescope gives you something at the same time that it takes something away. Without my telescope, I can see all the kids at once. You know, I get the big picture. If I use my telescope, I can see one or two kids much more clearly. What I gain in detail, I lose in range."

"Awesome!" I said, enjoying how Mr. Rodriguez talked to me like I was a grown-up.

"Well, Paige," he asked finally, sitting on the edge of his desk, "did you turn in an outline yet, and the draft of your paper?"

"No, the draft of our paper was due today, but I just finished my research now."

"Do you have enough notes to write a good paper?"

"Well, I don't have very many notes at all," I said, looking at a whole bunch of messy pages in front of me. Mostly I had drawn little pictures while I was thinking about some of the stuff I read. There were a few words on the pages, but they were kind of hard to see because of all the little drawings. I thought sadly of Jessica's carefully-organized research.

"May I look?" asked Mr. Rodriguez, holding out his hand.

"Sure, I guess so," I picked up the first few sheets and handed them to him.

Mr. Rodriguez stared at my pages, then sat up straight to examine them more closely. "These are *very* good," he said, as if surprised.

Now it was my turn to act surprised. "My notes? Even I can hardly read the words."

"Not your words," he said, "but your drawings. They're very interesting, very creative. I've read about this way of recording what you read, Paige, but I've never seen anyone actually do it. I'm impressed."

"You are? You can have them if you want."

"May I?" He seemed pleased. "Maybe later. If you give them to me now you won't have any notes to write your paper with. I know you said you have problems remembering things. How will you remember everything you've learned?"

"That's okay," I said. "I don't need any notes. I remember this stuff. It's easy because it's . . . . I don't know . . . . interesting. I really liked reading about stars. I mean, there are some totally awesome things in outer space, like the red giants and the white dwarfs and the pulsars and the black holes. I'm going to write my paper this weekend. There's so much to write about, it should be easy!"

"Well, how about if you take these notes for now and give them back to me after the contest?" said Mr. Rodriguez.

"Oh, all right. But this star paper's going to be so easy now that I've done my research."

"Why don't you tell me about it?" he said, settling back into his comfortable desk chair.

"Well it's like this: All stars start out in nebulas, which are .... um .... clouds of gas and dust. Some of them begin to come together because of gravity and begin to stick together harder and harder which makes it hotter and hotter and eventually it just catches on fire." I waved my hands in the air to show him. "When that happens, a star is formed."

"Good! Can you tell me more?"

"Well, stars with medium and big amounts of mass, or stuff, turn into supernovas! Do you know what they are?"

"Yes, I do. But why don't you tell me in your own words instead?"

"Well, I think they're like these awesome .... explosions of light and color and gas and dust. The star loses most of what it's made of in the explosion but, wow, is it beautiful! All stars are burning out, you know, even the little ones. Every one of them will die off. But if I were a star, I would hate to just fade away like the ones that don't have a lot of mass do. I'd want to go out in a beautiful big bang like a supernova!"

"Is that what this is, a supernova?" Mr. Rodriguez pointed to one of the pictures on my notes.

"Yeah," I said. "But I'm not finished. There's more."

"Okay. I'm listening." After I finished describing pulsars and black holes, he said, "Your paper should be very interesting!"

"If you were my teacher, would you give me a good grade on it?" I asked hopefully.

"Well, I'd have to see it first," he replied. "But if you gave me an outline which went over what you just told me, I'd give you a good grade on that part. How is yours coming along, anyway?"

"Oh, that!" I said, suddenly nervous. "I don't need to do an outline. It's all in my head. So I'm just going to write the paper."

"Don't discount the value of an outline, Paige," Mr. Rodriguez began. "It's very helpful to organize your thoughts and to . . . . "

"Anyway," I broke in quickly, "you should see my three-dimensional illustrations!" I told him about all the glittery stars in my garage. "They came out really awesome. I wish you could see them."

"I'd like to," he said. "Tonight I'm visiting Frank again. Maybe I'll call your mom and ask her if it's okay to stop by and take a look. You'd better get back to class right away."

I nodded and left, so excited about his coming over that I left my notes under a book on his table.

That evening when he came, I made everyone wait outside until I had all my stars plugged in. Then I turned off the light in the garage. "You can come in now!" I called out.

Mom held the door for him as he stepped in carefully.

"Wow!" he exclaimed, surveying my display. "Paige, this is fantastic!"

Mom looked at me and flashed a big smile.

Mark had followed Mom, and he chimed, "Awesome! Can I play with it? Please, Paige, please!"

"No, honey!" Mom said quickly. "Paige made this to take to school next week. It's her homework."

"Oh, man!" said Mark. "How come I never get homework like that?"

"You're in kindergarten," I said. "You don't get homework at all." Mom and Mr. Rodriguez laughed.

"I'll bet *nobody* else has homework like this!" said Mr. Rodriguez. "Paige, you completely outdid yourself. I think Mrs. Bourgeois is going to be very surprised. I'm not sure that she's expecting you to have done this much."

98

"Paige seems very determined to win this competition," said Mom.

"Your daughter has worked persistently on this assignment, Mrs. Bradley," the assistant principal said. "You should be very proud of her."

"Oh, I am," said Mom, ruffling my hair. "She is pretty special. . . . It's just that . . . . well, only one child will get to present a paper. I hope she's not too disappointed if someone else wins the competition."

"Oh, Mom," I said quickly. "No one else can win! I've just got to meet Dr. Kelsey!"

"Dr. Kelsey, Dr. Kelsey!" said Mom laughing. "All I hear about is Dr. Kelsey. You're counting on this so much, sweetie! I would hate for you to be let down."

"Mo-om!" I wailed, embarrassed by the way she was making her doubts so obvious.

Mr. Rodriguez and Mom exchanged looks, then he said, "Well, I have to be going now. Thanks for showing me, Paige. It's terrific."

After he left, I decided to forgive Mom for not believing in me. After all, she just didn't understand how determined I was to win. All that was left to do was to write the paper.

"Paige, Mark," Mom said, entering the house, "time to get ready for bed."

"I'm going to set my alarm for five o'clock in the morning," I said from the couch as I pulled off my sneakers.

"Why on earth would you do that?" asked Mom.

"I have to. I want to get an early start on my paper."

"Well," she replied, guiding Mark toward the bathroom for his bath, "Just don't wake up Mark!"

"No problem," I said. "I'll be quiet as . . . . Mousie!" That was the last laugh I had before several days of the hardest work I've ever done.

11

In A Time Warp

Brrrrrrng! When the Sailor Moon clock on my night stand sounded, its red numbers gave off the only light in my dark room. I rolled over, smacked the button, then dozed off again.

Clang, clang . . . whoosh. Three hours later, I woke up again to the typical Saturday morning sounds of Mom banging pots and pans and water running in the kitchen. I sat up in bed to find the room bright with sunlight and Mark's bed empty.

Oh no, my paper! I thought. Oh well, no rush. After all, there were six more days till the deadline.

I got up, dressed, and went to the kitchen for breakfast.

"Good morning," said Mom. "I made apple pancakes. Will you please set the table?"

Mark came into the kitchen and sat down, already dirty from playing outside.

"Hey, Paige," he said. "Is it okay for me to go into the garage now? I just want to look at your homework."

"No way."

"Oh, please," he pleaded. "I won't touch anything, honest. I promise."

I was relieved when Mom came to my rescue, saying, "Mark, don't pester your sister. Her project is very important to her, and for now the garage is off limits."

"No fair!" protested Mark.

"If you wait until after next week," I said in a burst of generosity, "I'll let you play with it—but only when I'm right beside you. Okay?"

"Yeah, sure! Thanks!" Mark brightened up.

"Paige, will you be working on your paper today?" Mom asked.

"Yep!"

"Do think you can do your work in the living room? Betty Willis is coming over, and she's going to help me refinish this," she said, patting our kitchen table.

"Sure. But why do you need Mrs. Willis to help you?"

"Betty is very good at restoring and refinishing furniture. She redid most of the pieces in her house, and they look great. And, of course, my background is in antiques. . . . I probably shouldn't say anything about this yet, we're still just talking about it, but . . . ." Mom hesitated. "We're thinking about starting our own antique furniture restoration business. What do you think of that?"

"Wow!" I said. "I'd be really proud of you."

"Well, we'll see what happens," she said, but I could tell she felt more excited than she let on.

After breakfast, I got out some paper, found a pencil, cleared off the coffee table, and arranged my things in an attractive design. I surveyed my supplies. Where to begin the writing? While my mind explored possible starting points, I picked up the pencil and studied it. What a dull point! I can't possibly start a big project with a dull pencil, I thought, and rose to sharpen it.

I went into the kitchen counter and stuck the pencil in the sharpener. Vroommmmmm! Wow, did it work fast! Pulling out my pencil to examine it, I was disappointed to find the point broken off completely. I tried again, but next time the point was flat. After several more tries, there was nothing left! I threw it away.

Following a juice break, I began searching for another pencil, and then realized I had probably just destroyed the last one in the whole house. "Mom," I called out from the kitchen, "I need a pencil, and we don't have any."

"Look in the drawers under the microwave!" Mom called from inside the hall closet where she was rummaging.

"I did."

"Then look in my purse," she said, her voice muffled.

Just then the front doorbell rang. "Oh, hi, Mrs. Willis," I said, letting our neighbor in.

"Hi, Betty," said my mom, coming out of the closet. "Let's go into the kitchen. I'll make some coffee."

Finally, I found a nice sharp pencil in my mom's purse and sat down on the floor in front of my report again. Well, actually, I thought, it wasn't a report yet. It was just a blank, white pile of paper.

Wanting to fill the blankness before it overwhelmed me, I wrote my name on the top. Then, remembering Jessica's remarks about my messy handwriting, I crumpled it and tossed it underneath the coffee table.

Taking a new sheet of paper off the pile, I wrote my name again. That looked better! But the paper still looked pretty empty.

So I wrote the date.

Then I stared at my paper. What else was supposed to go at the top?

I know! I thought, I'll give it a title! "Stars," I wrote in the center of the third line. This was progress now!

Half an hour later, I had to admit that the heading was the easiest part. Where should I start when everything I'd read seemed to be connected in a big, moving circle? All the facts I'd learned had to do with stars. But then again, they were all different.

"Think, Paige!" I said out loud, staring at my very blank, very white pile of paper. Maybe I should start with the new stars themselves. But, no, if I did that, I'd have to begin in three different places at once because stars of

different masses had different things happen to them. Maybe I could work better after taking a break. I wondered if any good cartoons were on.

Mark must have had the same thought because just then he burst through the front door, slamming it shut behind him. He turned on the television set and collapsed on the couch.

"Hey, cat turd," I said, "can't you see I'm working here? Go away!"

"I just want to see what's on," he said, grabbing the remote and flipping channels.

"Try channel twelve," I said, disgustedly.

"Okay. Hey, look! *Ocean Wizard* is on!"

I looked. "Must be a rerun," I said, getting up slowly and going over to sit next to him on the couch. "But this *was* a good one. You gotta agree to turn the TV off right after *Ocean Wizard,* because I have to write my paper in here. Okay?"

Mark didn't answer me. His eyes already had that glazed-over, television-watching look.

Lakesha and Kenyatta Willis joined us towards the end of that show, and we were halfway through *Puppernickel, the Wonder Dog,* when Mom let out a yell from the kitchen. "Mark! Come here right now!"

She's finally opened up the middle leaf of the kitchen table and uncovered Mark's personal compost pile, I thought, running into the kitchen after my brother. Sure enough, the peas and other food he'd collected would have made an interesting science fair project about weird mold. I headed back to watch some more *Puppernickel,* but Mrs. Willis poked her head in after me.

"You kids turn off that TV set and go out and play. You're rotting your brains!"

"Aww," Lakesha protested, then got up to obey. "Come on, Kenyatta. Come on, Paige. Let's go outside."

"I can't," I said. "I have homework to do."

"Well, bye, then," said Kenyatta. They left.

By this time it was noon. I took a lunch break, knowing I needed plenty of energy to start such a big job.

After lunch, I sat down in front of the coffee table and stared at my paper again, still wondering where to start. Uncomfortable sitting up, I stretched out on the floor to think. I stared at the ceiling, pretending to gaze at stars like Mr. Rodriguez did. There was a nebula spinning off billions of brand new shiny stars. They whirled around overhead in a carousel of star births and star deaths. Starting to feel sleepy, I imagined Dr. Kelsey and Captain Stone riding the carousel of dancing stars. It was so pretty, I drifted off.

"Paige, wake up," Mom said, bending over me to shake my shoulder. "It's dinner time."

"Dinner!" I sat up, yawning. "Where's Mrs. Willis?"

"She went home. Now come and eat."

"But I have to write my paper!"

"Well, you can get started again after dinner."

"Okay," I sighed, following her into the kitchen. "I'm having such a hard time getting the first paragraph!"

"Well," said Mom, "if I were you, I'd just write the first thing that comes into my head. If you just write anything down, the rest may come to you. You can always change the order of your ideas later when you rewrite what you've written.

"Just don't quit," she continued, smiling. "Use some of that persistence of yours, and make Dr. Kelsey proud!"

12

Canine Invader

On Saturday night I took up my post in front of the pile of blank paper while Mom and Mark played Monopoly in the kitchen. I decided to try out Mom's suggestion and write the first thing that came into my head. I stared at the paper, ready to seize upon my first thought. The first thing that I thought of was . . . . ice cream. I wanted some ice cream. And not just any ice cream, I wanted Brocato's ice cream. I wish Dad were here, I thought. He would have taken us to Brocato's. But Dad was on a trip in Las Vegas. He had promised to bring us souvenirs. What would they be? Hey, wait a minute! I stopped myself. Stars, Paige! Think stars!

I picked up my pencil. I would write something I knew about the stars. I would just write anything.

"Nebulas," I wrote, "are clouds of gas and dust."

Great! I had a sentence. Feeling better, I tried again. "Stars are born in nebulas."

No, that was dumb. I crossed out the words "are born."

Stars are not born. They are made. No, that's not right either. They just happen. I crossed out the whole sentence and wrote:

"Stars happen in nebulas."

But that didn't sound right either. Feeling terribly sleepy, I rested my head on my arms. It was hopeless. I decided to go to bed early and try again on Sunday.

After church the next day, we ate lunch. When we were finished, I sat down in front of my paper again.

After awhile, Mom came into the living room. "How's it going?"

"Terrible," I admitted. "But I'm going to finish the rest of this today."

Hours later, when I saw the street lights come on through the living room window, I threw down my pencil in disgust. I didn't have the heart to stare at those same two sentences anymore. I picked up all the crumpled balls of paper under the coffee table as well as all the paper around the wastebasket and tossed them into the wastebasket.

Then I went into the kitchen. "Mom, can I go outside?" She looked up from the classified ads she was reading in the Sunday paper. Mark was lying on the floor with the funny pages spread out around him.

"Where are you going?" she asked.

"I bet she's going to go climb that dumb old tree again," he said, then added, "Somebody who looks as much like a monkey as you ought to stay out of trees. They're going to catch you and put you in the zoo. You'll have to spend the night there before Mom and I can convince them you don't belong!"

I glared at him, but before I could reply, Mom said, "Cut it out, Mark. Go ahead, Paige. Just come back in before it gets too dark."

As I opened the back door, a familiar frantic barking sounded from around the side of the house: Peevers.

"Mom," I stuck my head back in the door. "Better come out. Sounds like Peevers is in trouble again."

"What am I going to do with that dog?" Mom sighed, getting up and following me out.

"I'll get the newspaper," yelled Mark, hopping to his feet, too.

I suddenly realized with horror where the sound was coming from.

"Mom, come quick!" I yelled. "Peevers is in the garage!" We all bolted out of the house. Mom passed me and reached the garage door first, pulled it open, and fumbled for the light switch.

Mark followed and said, "There's Fishbreath!" The

cat was pacing back and forth in front of a pile of old furniture stacked in the corner of the garage. Tufts of dog fur clung to the scattered remnants of my once-beautiful stars, while a length of twine that I had hung them on was now tangled around one of the cat's paws. Fishbreath herself was covered with glitter. A strand of broken Christmas tree lights trailed out from underneath a table in the corner, where Peevers cowered, barking and howling.

"Peevers, Fishbreath, what did you *do?*" I wailed.

"Oh, Paige, honey, I'm *so* sorry!" Mom said, surveying the damage. "Where is that dog? I can hear her, but I can't see her. How did these animals get in here? The garage door was closed."

"I didn't do it!" said Mark, too quickly.

"What didn't you do?" asked Mom, turning to him.

"I didn't come in here just to look at Paige's homework and accidentally forget to close the door," he said in a little, scared voice.

"Oh, Mark . . ." Mom began reproachfully.

"I'm sorry!" he said, tears forming in his eyes. "I didn't mean to do it, Paige! I'm really sorry! It was just too hard to wait until next week . . . ." His voice trailed off, and he started to sob.

"It's okay," I said in a low voice. Yelling at him

wouldn't bring back my beautiful stars. Besides, I didn't have a paper to go with them, anyway.

Peevers began to howl mournfully. Although it was dark under the table, I could just make out Mousie lying on the cement floor of the garage next to a chocolate brown paw.

"Peevers! What am I going to do with you?" Mom threw up her hands. Fishbreath hissed. I knew what *she* wanted to do with Peevers. This time, I agreed.

I didn't wait to watch Mom drag Peevers out. Too heartbroken to feel interest in anything, I left and headed straight for my bedroom. Once in bed, I pulled the covers over my head and started to cry. Jessica and Pauline were going to laugh at me when I didn't have a paper or any illustrations to turn in. There were only five days until the winner was selected, and I had nothing to show for the last two weeks of work. I had no chance of meeting Dr. Kelsey now. I cried myself to sleep.

13
Brain Telescope

On Monday morning, Breanna and I were working in the science center on a model of the solar system. We were painting a white Styrofoam ball to look like the planet Mars. The problem was that Keith had wanted to do Mars, but instead Mrs. Bourgeois assigned Venus to him and Will Schiffer. That was a bad move because Keith and Will thought that Venus was a sissy planet. As a result, they had decided to make our lives miserable. They consoled themselves by flicking little drops of paint at us every time Mrs. Bourgeois turned around.

"I don't care," said Breanna finally, fed up. "They're about to get Mars, all right. I'm going to throw it at them."

Just then a fat blob of blue paint landed on Breanna's nose. I giggled, despite myself, but she really was mad.

"I'm sorry," I said, stifling my laugh.

"That's it!" said Breanna, shoving her chair back and standing up. "I'm going to tell Mrs. Bourgeois."

I watched her go, then turned to see what Keith and

Will were doing. They were looking up at the ceiling and whistling, pretending that somebody else had thrown the paint.

I rolled my eyes and returned to our Mars model. Suddenly my lap felt wet. Looking down, I gasped to see my leg covered with bright red liquid. Oh, no, I thought, I'm bleeding!

"Paige knocked the paint over!" Keith yelled. Paint? The can was lying on its side. I wasn't hurt after all. But I could have died of embarrassment!

Luckily, it was water soluble paint that came off in the girls' room. Mrs. Bourgeois gave me an extra change of clothes that she kept in her desk for emergencies: a pair of jeans and a T-shirt that said, "Goombay Summer," whatever that means.

I was walking back to the classroom when suddenly I decided to go see Mr. Rodriguez. I knocked on his door.

"Come in," he called. Seeing me, he asked, "How's your paper going?"

"There is no paper," I said. "I'm a failure." I told him then about what happened to my stars and how I had only written two lines after working the whole weekend. "Getting to meet Dr. Kelsey is the most important thing in the world to me. I worked so . . . . hard . . . . (I slowed down because my lip was trembling), but it just proves what everybody says: I must really be dumb after all."

"I thought we discussed this before," said Mr. Rodriguez. "You're definitely not dumb. It is a real shame about your stars, but, you know, all you actually have to do to satisfy Mrs. Bourgeois is provide illustrations for your

paper. I know you can draw those."

"Yeah, well, I have to have a paper first. If I can't write it, I can't illustrate it."

"From what you told me on Friday, it sounds like you know your subject very well," said Mr. Rodriguez. "Why do you think it's so hard to write it all down?"

"I don't know. I guess it's because when I think about

everything I read, I have too many ideas at once. I mean I see how it all kind of works together, you know, like all these connections between the different types of stars and things like that. I feel like I'm exploding with thoughts. Kind of like a supernova—you know what I mean—" I waved my hands in the air, "with ideas and possibilities flying out of my head in all directions."

"But that's not the whole problem," I continued. "Then, I want to follow each and every idea . . . . at the same time." I laughed, embarrassed.

"Supernova describes you perfectly, Paige." Mr. Rodriguez laughed, too. "By the way, seeing so many connections that you don't know where to start describes an ADD kid, too. I think ADD is getting you down."

"Who cares about ADD at a time like this? I just need to write this paper." My voice wavered.

"Maybe you need some tools."

"What kind of tools?" I said, my eyes roaming around the room before settling on his telescope. Then, all of sudden, I had a really wild thought. "I know!" I said, slowly. "I need a brain telescope. It's like I'm either stuck on the big picture or lost in the details. I need something that can help me to focus on what I need to do at the moment. Do you have any brain telescopes in here, Mr.

Rodriguez?" I asked, half jokingly.

"Not exactly," he said. "But there are tools you can use to get similar results. For example, outlining—don't make that face!" he said, laughing. "Outlining is a tool that many people use to help themselves organize their thoughts. Why do you hate it so much?"

I sighed, "I don't know. Writing an outline just seems harder than writing the paper. And writing the paper is completely impossible!"

He laughed again, then said, "Don't look so miserable, Paige! Sit down, and I'll guide you through an outline for your paper."

"Oh, would you really?" I said, relieved.

"I said *guide,*" Mr. Rodriguez emphasized. "You're going to do the work yourself. I'm just going to provide encouragement. You can do this, Paige. I know you can." Despite my horrible weekend, something in his voice made me think that maybe I could.

"Okay. Ready." I sighed.

We worked on the outline for about half an hour, weaving in ideas from the words and pictures on my notes. Mr. Rodriguez said it was like making a skeleton of my final paper and that once I'd finished it, I could add the body parts by myself at home. When we were done, I couldn't believe it. I actually had an outline that I had done myself, with coaching from Mr. Rodriguez, of course. I felt so proud.

That evening, my astonishment grew as I continued working on my paper at home. Mr. Rodriguez was right! The outline was like having a list of all the things I had to include in my paper.

I was just drifting off to sleep when an amazing thought caused me to sit straight up in bed: It was Monday night, and I had actually forgotten to watch *Star Warrior!* Oh, well, I thought, lying down again and pulling the sheet up to my neck. This week, I'll just have to ask Dr. Kelsey herself what happened! Cheered by this thought, I drifted off to sleep.

The next morning I practically danced into the assistant principal's office before school. "Look, Mr. Rodriguez! My paper. It's done!"

He grinned at me over a thick stack of mail he was working on. "That's terrific! Your first draft, huh?"

"My first draft? . . . No, you don't understand," I said. "This is my *paper."*

"Well, I haven't read that paper yet," he said, "but just in case you don't know, let me tell you about two other writers' tools called rewriting and proofreading . . . . "

At that point, I knew better than to argue with him. "Okay." I sat down, sighing heavily. "Tell me."

Wednesday night I rewrote the entire paper more neatly, made my sentences sound better, and added some other stuff that I had forgotten to include the first time.

Thursday night while I was double-checking the spelling of all the hard words in my paper, there was a knock on the front door.

"It's Kelly LeBlanc!" I joined Mark at the door, where Kelly was standing with a brand new gray toy mouse in her right hand.

"Here," she said, handing it to me. "My mom bought this at the supermarket for Peevers."

Mom, coming up behind me, chuckled and said, "Tell your mother I said thank you very much."

"Here, Peevers!" I called, and she came bounding around the corner of the house. Mom tore off the wrapping and tossed her the mouse.

Peevers was ecstatic. You would have thought that she had been given a tyrannosaurus-size bone. Right away she took her new toy out to the back yard and buried it. Then she dug it up and buried it again. And again. And again. I guess she really is persistent. Like me.

14
Clouds of Gas and Dust

The Friday we were to turn in our papers dawned bright with promise, starting exactly according to my plan. I remembered to set my alarm and got up on time. Mom made scrambled eggs for us. I was so nervous about forgetting my paper that I checked my backpack five times to make sure it was there. Unfortunately, the fifth time I checked, I couldn't find it. I panicked. But then Mom showed me where it was, stuck in my math folder.

Still, I kind of lost track of time getting ready and missed the bus. Good old Mom drove me to school in time to play with Breanna on the playground before the bell rang. Then it was time to line up and go inside.

When we got settled in the classroom, Mrs. Bourgeois called the roll and then sent Carol around to collect our research papers. "I expect to spend most of the day grading these reports." Mrs. Bourgeois went on. "I'd prefer not to have to do this during class time. But the assembly is Monday, and I'd like the student who will be presenting his or her paper to have the weekend to prepare for it. In any event, I have some worksheets and other assignments to keep you busy while I work on these."

"When will you announce who has the highest grade?" asked Will.

"At the end of the day," said Mrs. Bourgeois.

A few moments later, Carol paused in the aisle. "Yuck! Mrs. Bourgeois, I don't have to touch *that,* do I?" Everybody looked to see what she was talking about. She was standing next to Keith's desk, and he was trying to hand her his report, which was a one-page sheet of paper stiff with mud.

"I kind of dropped it on the way to school," said Keith, grinning at Carol's discomfort.

"Just bring it to the front of the room yourself, Keith," Mrs. Bourgeois sighed.

All afternoon, I tried to concentrate on the boring worksheets, but my mind kept straying to the image of Dr. Kelsey standing on the stage at Probst Elementary. Who would be next to her? At 2:30 I looked around the room. How strange! Right now, every single kid in here still had a chance to be the one on the stage with Dr. Kelsey. But in thirty minutes, there would be one winner and sixteen losers sitting here. Well, that's not exactly true, I thought, remembering the stars that Peevers and Fishbreath destroyed. Every single kid doesn't really have a chance. I probably don't. Then, I remembered Keith's one-page, messy paper. It wasn't *much* comfort, but he probably didn't stand a chance either.

Was Keith worried? I wondered, looking across the aisle at him. He seemed supremely unconcerned, occupying himself by flicking paper spitballs into the back of Carol's thick brown hair. Will Schiffer, who sat on the other side of him, was giggling and urging him on. Carol worked away on her assignment, completely unaware of the blizzard of paper dots she was wearing.

Not knowing whether to envy Keith's unconcern, I admitted to myself that Jessica or Pauline stood a fair chance of truly winning. Mom was right; I shouldn't have counted on having the prize for myself. Well, maybe there'd be a miracle. It seemed like the suspense would never end.

Finally Mrs. Bourgeois straightened the pile of reports and stood up. Here it comes, I thought, holding my breath.

"Okay, class," the teacher began, "if you haven't finished your worksheets, take them home. I've decided not to give you any other homework this weekend. Please gather your belongings, and when you're ready, I'll announce the name of the student with the winning report and give the rest of you your grades."

Disappointed by the delay, I let my breath out. Mrs. Bourgeois turned calmly and began erasing the blackboard. As my classmates began to move about, I could feel excitement in the air like electricity. I don't think that fourth graders ever packed up so fast! Jessica and Pauline glanced at each other, smiling and crossing their fingers confidently, but I felt sick.

Finally Mrs. Bourgeois finished erasing the board and dusted chalk off her hands. "Okay, now if everyone's ready . . . ." She picked up the stack of papers from her desk and thumbed through them. I sucked in my breath again.

"Now, boys and girls," she began finally, "I just want to let you all know that I appreciate how hard you worked on these papers. . . . I can honestly say that I haven't received work of this quality in a long time. I wish we had a television star visitor every month!" She chuckled at her own joke. But nobody laughed; we were all too nervous.

I exhaled again, wondering if she would ever get to the point. My heart was pounding so loud I almost couldn't hear her voice. I sat straight up in my seat and watched her.

She cleared her throat and went on. "As I was saying, most of these papers were very, very good. I was very pleased. In fact, they were so good that ten of you got an 'A' and three earned 'A pluses.' One of those three students is going to present her paper at the assembly. I say 'her' because all of the three top papers in this class were written by girls."

"Aww," the boys moaned their disappointment. "That's not fair!"

"Actually, I had to make a very difficult decision with respect to those three papers," Mrs. Bourgeois went on.

"Who were the girls?" Pauline's voice came out in a rather impatient squeak. She sounded nervous, too.

"Well one of the three 'A pluses' went to . . ." She peered through her glasses at the pile of papers in her hand. "Breanna Barnett. Breanna did a very good paper on the Planet Pluto with excellent illustrations from her computer."

Hooray! I reached forward and tugged at my friend's ponytail. She flashed me an exultant grin.

"The next paper was also very good. It belonged to Jessica Patino." I heard a squeal from behind me. "In fact, Jessica did something very clever. She wrote to Astronaut Sally Ride for information. Dr. Ride wrote back, and the result was a very good paper."

What? I thought, glaring at Jessica. That was my idea!

Jessica avoided my eyes, but she had a big grin on her face.

"Of the three best papers, one of them was clearly the best. And that is the last paper I have here."

She looked directly at me. My heart leaped, and I discovered I was holding my breath again.

"That was your paper, Paige," she said. "You packed in *so much* information, and you had these wonderful, hand-drawn illustrations that are informative as well as beautiful."

"Oh!" My breath forced itself past my lips as if someone had pounded me on the back. I won? I don't think I'd ever felt happier in my life than I did at that moment. I could hardly believe it.

Everybody started talking at once. Breanna turned around and gave me a smile as radiant as the sun.

"I don't believe it," Jessica yelped.

"Now, wait a minute! Be quiet, please! I'm not finished." Mrs. Bourgeois looked dismayed.

While everyone quieted down, I studied the teacher's face. In a flash, I knew right away that something was very wrong.

"I had a very difficult decision with respect to your paper, Paige," she said, looking at me with a pained expression. "It was clearly the best . . . . but what I'm trying to say is that . . . . I can't let you present it at the assembly."

Silence fell as if all sound had been sucked away from the room. My stomach ached as if she had just punched me. I sat unmoving, numb.

"I'm sorry," she began again. "This has been a very difficult decision, but you didn't follow all the rules. Everyone else—well, almost everyone—" she corrected herself, glancing at Keith, "turned in their outlines and rough drafts, which were necessary to complete the project. You didn't. I'm sorry, but I have decided that the next-best paper will be presented instead at the assembly. That's yours, Jessica."

Just then the bell rang. The room erupted into noise as the kids grabbed their books and dashed toward the front of the room.

"Pass my desk, please, and pick up your papers on the way out!" Mrs. Bourgeois shouted over the din.

I sat perfectly still in my seat, staring straight ahead, while the classroom emptied. Feeling a hand on my shoulder, I looked up to see Breanna.

"Hey," I said softly before she could open her mouth. "I'm *really* glad you got an 'A plus.'" Somehow, I managed to smile at her. "You should be up on that stage, not Jessica. You did everything right, and you deserve it."

"Thanks. I'm sorry . . . . " she started and then stopped as I shook my head, brushing away tears. "See you Monday, huh?" Giving me a sympathetic smile, she headed for the door.

"Yeah, see you Monday," I echoed. Rising stiffly like a robot, I picked up my backpack and approached Mrs. Bourgeois' desk for my paper.

She didn't look up from the work she was doing. I reached down to take the paper, but my fingers wouldn't open to pick it up. Mrs. Bourgeois' silver hair blurred because of the tears in my eyes so that I couldn't see which paper was mine.

Fairies dancing on her head, I thought with disgust. If I wasn't always wasting time imagining such dumb stuff I could've done the stupid outline *and* written the best paper.

Finally, she looked up at me. "Paige, are you okay?"

Suddenly I realized I didn't really want my old report. I left it lying there as I hurried out of the classroom, running straight into Jessica, who was standing just outside in the hall. Waiting for me, maybe.

"Hey, Paige," she said. She looked uncomfortable. "I, um, I'm really sorry that . . . . um . . . . well, I think that it wasn't fair the way Mrs. Bourgeois told you that in front of the whole class. . . ." Jessica sounded like she was truly trying to be nice to me.

But I didn't care anymore; I was too mad. "You took my idea," I said, cutting her off.

"Well, you *could* have done it yourself!" she retorted, suddenly sounding like the Jessica I knew again. "In fact, you *said* you already wrote to Sally Ride. That's what gave me the idea. Anyway, I just wanted to say that I'm glad you got an 'A plus' and I don't know . . . I mean, I kind of feel sorry for you . . ."

"You feel *sorry* for me? You copied *my* idea to win, and now you feel *sorry* for me?"

I didn't wait to hear anything else she had to say; I just started to run—down the hall, out the front door, and down the steps. I hit the sidewalk without breaking my stride, and kept going. At a gallop, I passed all of the parked school buses.

"Hey, kid, where ya goin'?" called Mr. Gene, the bus driver, but I was already approaching the corner. I headed onto Wilkins Street which intersects Milton after about five blocks. My heart was pounding and my breath was coming out in sobs, but still I kept running the rest of the way home.

I slowed down, finally, at my own front door. I yanked

it open, threw my backpack onto the living room floor, and slammed the door.

"Paige! What are you . . . ?" With a mop in her hand, Mom emerged from the bathroom, but I dodged her sympathetic questions on the way to my room. There, I threw myself on my bed and pulled up the covers.

Mom came in after me. "Paige Bradley! What on earth is going on?" I kept my face hidden, still gasping for breath.

"Paige, honey. Do you want to talk?" she asked. I didn't answer. Go away, I said silently, but she didn't. Finally, I pulled the covers up over my head.

Mom sighed, "Okay, Paige. If you decide you want to

talk to me, I'll be out here." She left the door of my room open just a crack.

Later, I could hear Mom and Mark eating dinner in front of the television. "Mark, please," I heard her say, "don't make a mess. We're expecting company tonight."

Company! I sat up in bed, knowing with a sinking feeling that it would be Mrs. Bourgeois. She was going to bring the paper I had left behind at school. Worse, she was going to tell Mom all about how I had the best paper which wasn't really the best paper because of my stupid forgetfulness. I couldn't write an outline or do rough drafts like everybody else in my stupid class. No matter how hard I worked, I still didn't do it right. Spacey Paige!

I looked around my room. Where was that portal to an alternate universe when you needed it most? "Hey, space kid!" I whispered. "Why settle for goofy stuff like school supplies? You can have a complete human being, namely, me. I won't eat much, I promise. Just open the portal a little bit. Maybe a little tear in the fabric of the space-time continuum." I waited a second, looking around the room to see if any aliens wanted to take me up on my offer. But nothing happened. "Aww, who cares?" I muttered. Flopping back on my bed, I buried my face under my pillow. Who would want a loser like me, anyway?

15
First Star I See

Right after the evening news ended, the doorbell rang, and I heard Mom talking to someone. I bolted out of bed, not wanting to be there when my teacher finished telling Mom about my most recent failure.

The curtain swaying in front of the open bedroom window attracted me. I'll run away, I thought, and blow up the school on my way out of town. I wondered how far China really was. In a flash I ran to the window, pushed out the screen and jumped from the sill onto the cool grass outside. Standing uncertainly for a moment, I wondered how to go about running away. The rustling leaves of my tree caught me eye and ear, and I decided to sit there while making a plan. I climbed quickly until I reached my hammock. I lay back in it, pulling the sides over myself to frustrate the mosquitoes.

"Boy, I really blew it," I said softly to the tree. I watched her topmost branches sway in the breeze as the sky beyond them turned rose-pink and lavender. A tear rolled down my cheek, then another and another. I felt the tree closing around me as if trying to comfort me, but it was no use. After all, it was just a dumb, stupid tree. I was through with imagining stuff. After all, my imagination just got me into trouble. I started to sob noisily.

"Paige, is that you up there?"

I jumped. Twisting around carefully, I peered down through the leaves to where Mr. Rodriguez stood at the base of the trunk. What was he doing here?

"Go away!" I said, not wanting him or anyone to see me like this.

"Paige, I'm coming up," he said. Wiping my face on my shirt, I watched him pick his way through spots that were too small for him.

"I guess climbing a tree is like riding a bike," he said. "You never forget how to do it." But the ascent took him a lot longer than it took me. I eyed him warily when he finally settled on a branch close to me.

"Your mom and Mrs. Bourgeois are worried about you," he said.

"Did Mrs. Bourgeois send you?"

"No, but she did tell me what happened. And since I was going over to Frank's tonight anyway, I just thought I'd stop by to see how you were doing."

"I guess I'm not doing too good." I started to cry again. "It's not fair! I tried awfully hard," I gasped through deepening sobs, "I really did. How come no matter what I do, I'm always such a loser?"

Mr. Rodriguez didn't say anything. He just sat there with this kind of sad look on his face as if he knew how I felt. The branches creaked, and the leaves rustled in a friendly way as the evening sky slowly darkened. It was changing from baby pink and lavender to that pretty dark red and purple that make you feel like something important is happening right before your eyes. But the tears in mine made the colors run together.

Mr. Rodriguez fished a wadded-up tissue from his back pocket. "Here, you look like you need this," he said. "It's clean."

I blew my nose. "It's just not fair!" I repeated, fiercely. "I deserve to present my paper at the assembly. Mine is the best. Mrs. Bourgeois said so! Not only that, but Jessica Patino certainly didn't deserve to win. Mrs. Bourgeois loved her idea about writing to Sally Ride, but that was *my* idea! Once I gave her the idea, all Jessica had to do was to follow through on it. This is so unfair!"

"I can understand how you would feel that way."

"You know what else isn't fair?" Mr. Rodriguez shook

his head. "It's just that . . . . well, *lots* of times I have good ideas. But they don't seem to mean anything because I can't follow through with them on time. The hard part for me is always carrying them out when I'm supposed to."

"I believe that it's harder for you than for most people—following through on ideas on a timely basis," the assistant principal replied.

"But this time, it should have been different!" I cried. "I don't understand. I tried as hard as I could. Why wasn't my work good enough?" I searched his face desperately for an answer.

"You know, *that* is all that counts," he said.

"What's all that counts? Trying? That's not what counts! Getting to present your paper to the school counts! An 'A' on your report card counts! Getting to meet Dr. Kelsey and winning a crysto-laser, that's what counts! Trying is just what the losers were doing before they lost."

"Well, what do you think the winners were doing before they won?" he asked mildly.

But I wasn't about to be reasoned with. "I did try!" I whispered fiercely. "But it doesn't matter. I'm still a failure! A real loser."

"Paige," said Mr. Rodriguez with a very serious look on his face. "I know you tried as hard as you could. I also

135

believe that results count, but there's more to this than you're seeing."

I glanced at him, startled.

"Look up," he said, pointing to the sky. "You're missing the big picture." I sighed and gazed up where he was pointing. He continued, "I bet you know a lot more about our universe now than you did before you started your paper. I bet you'll never look at the stars the same way again."

As he spoke, I squinted my eyes to see better. Like a faraway light turning on, a tiny bright star twinkled into existence in the night sky above, framed all around by the branches of my tree. The star sparkled serenely, a brilliant candle of encouragement.

I began to think out loud about what he had been saying. "I did my best; I know I did," I repeated, almost to myself. "I did exactly what I set out to do, I wrote the best paper . . . . but in the end it didn't matter because I didn't follow all the directions. It's kind of like what you were saying about your telescope. I was focusing too narrowly on writing the best paper, and I didn't pay enough attention to the big picture."

Mr. Rodriguez smiled at me, nodding as if I had revealed a major discovery.

"I think that's my problem! My focusing knob is broken. I either get stuck on the big picture or on the little details. I don't go back and forth very easily, do I?"

"No, but if Dr. Learner was right about you, there are tools you can use to compensate for your ADD," said Mr. Rodriguez. "You may not have the same kind of ADD as Mark does, but it seems to make just as big a difference in your life as it does in his. Mark is getting help for his. That's something he can be proud of. He's learning new tools from Dr. Learner."

"My father says that ADD is 'just an excuse . . . . '" I said, hesitantly.

"Well, it shouldn't be," said Mr. Rodriguez. "Why don't you just consider it an explanation, instead? If you know why it's harder for you to do some things than it is for other people to do them, you won't waste a lot of time trying to solve your problems by using the same old, ineffective methods. Instead, you can spend that same amount of time looking for other tools to use to compensate for your differences." His big words reminded me that he was the assistant principal. Nevertheless, he was someone I could trust.

"Do you think Dr. Learner *could* help me?" I asked. "You know, to fix my focusing knob?"

"Yes," said Mr. Rodriguez, "that's a good place to start. This paper is just one project. You'll have many more down the road, so you need to learn how to deal with your ADD." He smiled at me. "I'm sure with your persistence, creativity and supernova brain, you'll figure it out."

"But, why can't you help me more?"

"I'd like to, but I've spent a lot of time with you on this project, and I have a whole school full of kids who need me. Besides, when you get older I may not be nearby."

I looked at the assistant principal. He had the nicest look on his face. "Thanks for everything, Mr. Rodriguez," I said softly, meaning it with all my heart. "Oh, and Mr. Rodriguez . . . ."

"Yes, Paige?"

"There's a *huge* mosquito on your nose!"

"If you feel better now, kiddo . . . ." he said, slapping it hastily, "can we get down from here and go inside somewhere where these bloodsuckers can't reach us?"

"See you at the bottom!" I called, scrambling to the base of my tree. "Hey, Mr. Rodriguez! What's taking you so long?" I called up, teasing.

"I'm coming! I'm coming! Ouch!" said Mr. Rodriguez, slapping at another mosquito.

139

That Saturday when I visited my dad, we had a heart-to-heart talk over spumoni ice cream at Brocato's. I told him about how the kids called me "spacey" and about all the stuff that was so hard for me to do. I also told him about everything that had happened since my last visit with him, about how I'd both won and lost the contest at the same time, and about all that I had learned about myself. I told him I thought maybe I wanted to start seeing Dr. Learner to help me with my "broken focusing knob."

I was very nervous talking to Dad about all this because I thought he would tell me how wrong I was. But instead he replied, "Pumpkin, maybe you're right. Now, I want you to know that I like you just the way you are!" He paused to let this thought sink in, then continued, "But seeing this lady does seem to be helping your brother, and, who knows, it probably can't hurt!" Dad even said that he'd talk to Mom and offer to help pay for my visits to Dr. Learner! I surprised him by giving him a bone-crushing hug!

But the next day I got an even better surprise!

16
Mission Accomplished

On Monday morning, Jessica was completely impossible, just as I'd expected. She wore a brand new outfit, lipstick and nail polish, and she even had shiny red shoes with high heels! I have to admit, she did look pretty even though she could barely walk without falling over. The kids kept asking her if she was excited and what she was going to say to Dr. Kelsey, treating *her* like she was a celebrity! The whole thing just made me sick, so I ignored her as best I could. Unfortunately it was all going on in the row behind me, so it was kind of hard not to listen.

Jessica had the nerve to say that Dr. Kelsey was probably going to select her paper as the best in the school and that the "virtual crysto-laser was *virtually* hers!" Everybody laughed at her joke, except me and Breanna (and Keith, of course). It would serve her right, I thought, if she would trip going up the steps to the stage and fall flat on her face in front of the entire school.

We were in the middle of a math lesson when the

intercom above the clock began to crackle and hiss. Mrs. Landry's voice squawked from the speaker, "Mrs. Bourgeois, will you please send Paige Bradley to the office?"

"What did you do this time, Paige?" whispered Pauline is a snotty voice.

"Go ahead to the office, and hurry back," said Mrs. Bourgeois. "You don't want to miss the assembly."

When I got to the main office, Mr. Rodriguez was waiting for me, and Mrs. Landry was standing in front of her desk, smiling! I had never actually see her smile before, and it was kind of scary. When she reached out in a kindly way and patted me on the head, I almost fell over.

Mr. Rodriguez stood in the doorway to Mrs. Martin's office with a big grin. "Paige," he said, "come quickly. There's somebody here who wants to meet you." He seemed pretty excited and motioned to me to walk in. What was going on?

I entered slowly, not knowing who or what to expect.

Mrs. Martin, our principal, sat behind her desk with a big smile on her face. To my surprise, Mr. Hubble and several of the other teachers were standing there grinning like crazy, too. I almost didn't recognize them because they were all wearing suits today. The next thing I noticed was that there were two brown, padded chairs in front of Mrs. Martin's desk, and one was empty. On the edge of the other sat a tiny woman in a powder blue suit. She was wearing a corsage in our school colors, gold and purple. At her feet was a large silvery bag that looked kind of like a suitcase. Her face was very familiar.

But I still didn't know who she was until she said, "Hello, Paige." Then I knew in an instant! It was Dr. Kelsey.

She held out her graceful hand for me to shake. "I'm Renee La Straps. And I am *very* happy to meet you!"

I just stood there. What else was I supposed to do? I couldn't have been more surprised if Ed McMahon had told me I'd won the Publishers Clearinghouse Sweepstakes! My mouth hung open and I blinked several times to make sure I wasn't seeing things. . . . Yep, Dr. Kelsey was sitting there! My heart was pounding.

"Paige," said Mrs. Martin, nudging me, "Renee La Straps would like to shake hands with you."

I gulped, and then slowly reached out my hand to shake hers, my fingers brushing the huge diamond on her finger. I suddenly felt incredibly nervous!

"Sit down, please," Dr. Kelsey motioned to the empty chair. She looked around the room at all of the grown-ups standing around grinning. Then she turned to Mrs. Martin. "Carol," she asked, as if they were old friends, "I know we're on a tight schedule, but could I have a few minutes alone with Paige?"

"Why, certainly, Renee!" Mrs. Martin jumped to her feet, waved for everyone to leave. Mrs. Martin was the last one out, and she closed the door behind her, leaving me alone with Dr. Kelsey.

Leaning forward, Dr. Kelsey took my hands in hers. "Paige, I know you don't know me . . . ." she said.

Didn't know her? Of course I did! She was Dr. Kelsey!

She continued, "I heard that you are a very bright girl who has been diagnosed as having ADD. I mean, attention deficit disorder."

I know what it means," I said.

"I also heard," she continued, "that you think there's something wrong with getting treatment for your ADD. Is that true?"

"Well, not anymore," I said, regaining my voice at last. "My mother has been wanting me to go to see a doctor, and I've decided that I will."

She broke into a big smile. "Oh, I'm so glad to hear that! In fact, when your principal told me about you, I wanted to meet you to tell you how much treatment has helped my own little girl. Her name is Allegra. She's in Los Angeles right now in school, and she has ADD just like you. Ever since she's been getting treatment for it, she's felt much happier and can do many things that she couldn't before. Will you promise me that you won't change your mind about getting help for your ADD?" She looked at me earnestly.

Yes, I nodded, of course! I would have promised Dr. Kelsey anything!

"Good girl!" said Dr. Kelsey. "Now let me see . . . . hmm, I have a couple of my pictures in here," she reached down into the silver bag at her feet. "I'll autograph some of these for you if you would like."

"Oh, would you? I'd love it!" I watched her sign a picture of herself as Dr. Kelsey standing on the bridge of her star cruiser. She wrote: "To Paige, one of my favorite star-gazers! Keep your eyes on the skies, and best of luck! Love, Renee La Straps."

I decided to take a chance. "Dr. Kelsey," I asked breathlessly, "would you please sign another one for my friend Breanna, and one for my brother Mark?"

"Sure!" said Dr. Kelsey, signing two more. Then she reached down into her bag again and pulled out a shiny object. "I brought a few extra props with me. Would you like one of these?"

"A virtual crysto-laser! You bet!"

"All right then. It's yours!" She handed it to me, then she stood up and opened the door. "I'm so glad I was able to meet you! Good luck, Paige."

I shook Dr. Kelsey's hand one more time and drifted out of the room, backwards, accidentally bumping into Mr. Hubble. I blushed, but Dr. Kelsey laughed and waved to me. Waving back, I turned around and drifted back to my classroom, clutching my treasures.

As usual, when I opened the classroom door, everybody stopped what they were doing and looked up.

"Hey! Where'd you get that?" exclaimed Keith as I floated to my seat.

"I met her! I met Dr. Kelsey," I said. I still didn't believe it.

There was instant chaos in the room.

"You did what?"

"You met Dr. Kelsey!"

"No way!"

Everybody crowded around my desk.

"She gave me some autographed pictures . . . . and this," I said, triumphantly displaying the virtual crysto-laser. Pauline gasped.

Breanna turned around in her seat, smiling broadly. "I got this for you because you've been such a good friend," I said quietly, handing her the picture Dr. Kelsey had autographed for her.

"Oh, Paige! You're the best! Thanks!" Breanna bounced up and down in her seat, reading, " 'To Breanna,

all my love! . . . Renee La Straps.' Wow!"

Jessica's voice cut through the air with icy calm. "How did *you* get to meet her? That's not fair!"

This time I felt sorry for her. "I don't know!" I said trying to be kind. "She said she wanted to meet me! She's very nice. She's really short and much prettier than she looks on TV."

"I just don't believe it!" repeated Jessica.

"Oh, Paige, you are so lucky!" said Carol.

"Yeah, I guess so!" I said.

"All right, all right!" said Mrs. Bourgeois. "It's time to line up for the assembly, everybody. Jessica, don't forget your paper."

When we filed into the auditorium, Dr. Kelsey was already on the stage. I sat through all the presentations and the announcement of the overall winner while clutching my own virtual crysto-laser and autographed picture. Poor Jessica did not win the prize; a very short fifth-grader named Jordan Volpe did.

When we all filed out to go back to our classroom I waved to Dr. Kelsey, but she was signing autographs for some of the teachers and didn't see me. I shrugged it off because this had been the best day of my whole life, and nothing could ruin it.

When I got home and told Mom about the day, she was very happy for me. And when I gave Dr. Kelsey's autographed picture to Mark, he was so excited that he promised to let *me* have control of the television remote for an entire year!

Later that night, after dinner, Mrs. Willis came over. She and Mom sat at the kitchen table, which, by the way, looks great now that it has been refinished. They discussed names for their new business. I suggested "Supernova Antique Restoration," but they didn't like it too well. Nevertheless, it was still better than the name Mark had suggested, which was "Food Busters Antique Restoration."

Then I remembered what Dr. Kelsey had written on my autographed picture: To Paige, one of my favorite star-gazers! That gave me an idea. "Hey, Mom! What about Star-gazer's Antique Restoration?" I asked.

"Hmmm . . . . I like that," said Mrs. Willis slowly.

"What is a star-gazer?" asked Mark.

"It's another word for daydreamer," Mom replied. "It can also mean somebody who has his or her sights set pretty high, you know, somebody who seeks excellence. I like it too, Betty. It has a very nice ring as a name for our new business."

I went outside then, and climbed my tree. From the comfort of my hammock, I gazed through the branches to the stars, which sparkled and shone above me. It had been an amazing day! I still couldn't believe how lucky I'd been. Maybe my luck was finally changing.

But then I remembered Mr. Rodriguez saying, "Paige, there's still a lot of hard work ahead of you!"

I smiled and whispered out loud, "I know, I know! I'll

keep on trying to learn how to apply myself." But I don't mind so much because now I have some new tools. And I know where to find more.

Then a puzzling thought nearly sent me tumbling from my perch. After all the trouble my daydreams had caused me, Dr. Kelsey had called me one of her "favorite star-gazers." She must like daydreamers! Maybe it was good to be spacey sometimes! Once I fixed my focusing knob to control when to imagine and when to pay attention, then I could star-gaze any time I wanted.

Sinking back into my hammock, I smiled up at the night stars. And—was it *really* just my imagination?—they smiled back. ☆

More about ADD:

For Young Readers:
Eagle Eyes: A Child's Guide to Paying Attention, by Jeanne Gehret, M.A. (Fairport, New York: Verbal Images Press, 1990-1996) A picturebook for ages 6-10 by the publisher of *First Star I See.*

I'm Somebody Too, by Jeanne Gehret, M.A. (Fairport, New York: Verbal Images Press, 1992). A novel written from the viewpoint of the sister of "Eagle Eyes." For ages 9 and up.

Jumpin' Johnny, Get Back to Work! , by Michael Gordon, Ph.D. (DeWitt, New York: GSI Publications, 1991.) A picturebook about ADHD.

Learning to Slow Down and Pay Attention, by Kathleen Nadeau, Ph.D. (Annandale, VA: Chesapeake Psychological Publications, 1993). For grades 4-6.

My Brother's a World Class Pain: A Sibling's Guide to ADHD/Hyperactivity, by Michael Gordon, Ph.D. (DeWitt, New York: 1992). Addresses the feelings of brothers and sisters of children with ADD.

Putting On the Brakes: A Young People's Guide to Understanding Attention Deficit Hyperactivity Disorder, by Patricia O. Quinn, M.D. (New York: Magination Press, 1991) For Grades 3-6.

For Older Readers:

Women With Attention Deficit Disorder, by Sari Solden, MS, MFCC. (Grass Valley, California: Underwood Books, 1995). A book about what happens to girls with ADD (especially the non-hyperactive kind) when they grow up.

You Mean I'm Not Lazy, Stupid Or Crazy?!, by Kate Kelly & Peggy Ramundo. (Cincinnati: Tyrell & Jerem Press, 1993). A self-help book for adults with ADD.

Driven to Distraction: Recognizing and Coping with Attention Deficit Disorder from Childhood Through Adulthood, by Edward M. Hallowell, M.D. (New York: Touchstone, 1994).

About the Author:

Jaye Andras Caffrey was born and raised in New Orleans, Louisiana, where she graduated from Ursuline Academy, Tulane University, and Tulane University Law School. Currently, she works as an attorney and resides in Houston, Texas with her husband and two children, one of whom was recently diagnosed with ADD.

Despite the author's school achievements, her childhood was saddened by an undiagnosed attention deficit disorder. A voracious reader and incessant daydreamer as a child, she often felt lonely and confused. "I could never understand why the adults in my life were so frustrated with me," she recalls. Since her diagnosis at the age of thirty-one, she has found new ways to deal with the distractibility, disorganization, and loneliness once so evident in her life.

About the Illustrator:

Tracy L. Kane is an artist for Public Television, applying her skills from illustration to video to scenic design. She lives in New Hampshire with her husband and cat Nomi, who looks very much like Fishbreath!